POWER OF INT[U...]

CW00741100

Summary

Power Of Intuition

POWER, Volume 1

Hash Blink and Thomas sheriff

Published by Hash Blink & Rebellious Rebels LLC, 2024.

POWER OF INTUITION

First edition. February 27, 2024.

Copyright © 2024 Hash Blink and Thomas sheriff.

ISBN: 979-8224169733

Written by Hash Blink and Thomas sheriff.

Also by Hash Blink

POWER
Power Of Intuition

Standalone
The zodiac sign lover's
Hades
The immortal lover
The Wise Monkey
The forbidden idol

Watch for more at https://books.apple.com/us/audiobook/the-power-of-the-loner-discover-the/id1727418972.

Also by Thomas sheriff

POWER
Power Of Intuition

Standalone
The immortal lover
The Wise Monkey
The forbidden idol

Watch for more at https://books.apple.com/us/audiobook/the-male-hierarchy/id1727414547.

Table of Contents

In this horror novel, Tomas, a man of integrity and intuition, is called upon by his skeptical friend John to help with a malevolent presence in his home. As they confront the entity, they rely on their intuition and perform an incantation to banish it. However, Tomas soon discovers a summoning circle in his own apartment, indicating that someone has been trying to summon dark entities. With John's help, they banish the entity from Tomas's apartment as well. But their victory is short-lived as they realize the entity is still out there, growing stronger. They continue to face the entity, but their attempts to banish it become increasingly dangerous. In a final act of sacrifice, Tomas and John give their lives to banish the entity, leaving their friend Alex and psychic Lila to pick up the pieces. Together, they perform a ritual to banish the entity once and for all. However, they discover a cryptic message that hints at a deeper mystery. As they try to unravel the truth, a woman seeks their help, indicating that the malevolent presence may still be at large.

Alex and Lila, accompanied by Tomas, continue their investigation into the malevolent entity that has been haunting them. They receive guidance from Michael and his assistant Sophie, who provide them with amulets for protection. Despite taking a break to enjoy a day at the beach and finding solace in each other's company, they cannot escape the feeling of being watched. As they walk down a deserted street, they encounter the shadowy figure once again, leaving them on edge and
ready to confront the darkness that lies ahead.

As they ventured deeper into their quest, Alex, Lila, Tomas, and Marcus faced new challenges and encountered more dark entities. They relied on their intuition and the power of their amulets to protect themselves and uncover more artifacts. With each artifact they found, they felt a surge of hope, knowing that they were one step closer to defeating the darkness that threatened their world. However, they also became aware of a growing malevolence, a force that seemed to be orchestrating their every move. As they delved deeper into the darkness, they knew that they had to stay united and trust in their intuition, for it was their only hope in the
face of the daunting task ahead.

Tomas and his friends were relieved to learn that the darkness had been banished, but they now faced the challenge of understanding Tomas' newfound power. Michael explained that the power to control darkness had been passed down through Tomas' family for generations, but unlike his ancestors, Tomas had not been consumed by its darkness. This made him unique and presented an opportunity to use his power for good. Determined to understand and control his abilities, Tomas and his friends embarked on a journey of self-discovery and training, ready to
face whatever challenges lay ahead.

Tomas, overwhelmed with questions and no answers, is told by Michael that they must leave and prepare for the next challenge. As they step outside, they realize they have entered a new world full of mysteries and danger. Tomas feels a sense of foreboding but knows he must rely on his intuition to face the dangers ahead. They encounter a cursed village and learn about a witch's curse. Tomas's intuition sharpens as they delve deeper into the mystery, and he realizes there are other forces at play.

They face a battle with a terrifying creature and emerge victorious. They continue their journey, facing more dangers and relying on Tomas's intuition and newfound power. They encounter dark spirits, a grotesque creature, and a demon. They seek the demon's true name to command it to leave. Tomas confronts his darkest fear and finds the demon's name.

The journey continues, with more challenges ahead.

In this thrilling story, Tomas, Alex, and Lila embark on a dangerous journey to banish a powerful demon. With the help of their intuition and ancient artifacts, they successfully defeat the demon and continue their mission to rid the world of evil. Along the way, they face dark spirits, encounter a peaceful town, and discover more challenges that test their strength and determination. Despite the constant dangers, they rely on their intuition and the power of the artifacts to overcome each obstacle. Their journey is far from over, but they remain united and ready to face

whatever comes their way.

In Chapter 53, Tomas, Alex, and Lila find themselves in a dense fog surrounding a massive, gnarled tree. They can feel the darkness closing in on them, but they refuse to let fear overcome them. With their hands tightly clasped together, they step forward, ready to confront the source

of the darkness.

As they move through the fog, they hear whispers and see shadowy figures darting around them. The air is heavy with malevolent energy, but Tomas's intuition guides them forward. They know that they must stay focused and trust in their instincts if they are to overcome this final

challenge.

Suddenly, they reach a clearing, and the fog dissipates, revealing a towering figure standing before them. It is the embodiment of the darkness they have been fighting against. Its eyes glow with an eerie light, and its presence fills the air with a sense of dread.

Tomas, Alex, and Lila stand their ground, ready to face the darkness head-on. They draw their weapons and prepare for battle. With each strike, they feel the darkness weakening, but it fights back with a ferocity

they have never encountered before.

As the battle rages on, Tomas's intuition guides him to a hidden weakness in the darkness. He strikes with all his might, and the darkness lets out a deafening scream. It crumbles to the ground, defeated.

The trio stands victorious, their bodies battered but their spirits unbroken. They have finally vanquished the darkness that threatened their world. The village is saved, and a sense of peace settles over the land.

Tomas, Alex, and Lila return to the village as heroes, celebrated for their bravery and determination. They are hailed as the saviors who brought an end to the malevolent force that had plagued their world for so long.

But even as they bask in the adoration of the villagers, they know that their journey is not over. There are still other worlds to explore, other adventures to be had. With their intuition as their guide, they set off once again, ready to face whatever challenges lie ahead.

In this text, Tomas and his friends continue their journey to defeat the darkness that threatens their existence. They encounter various obstacles and face off against dark-cloaked figures, a demonic entity, a twisted woman, and more. Throughout their journey, Tomas relies on his intuition to guide them and make crucial decisions. They learn to trust each other and harness the power of their bond. Despite their victories, they remain vigilant, knowing that the darkness is still out there. They split up to cover more ground, with Tomas relying on his intuition to lead him to the darkness's weakness. As they approach the source of the darkness, the tension builds, leaving readers wondering if they will succeed in their mission.

Tomas and his friends continue their battle against the darkness, relying on their intuition and magical abilities to protect themselves and banish evil. They face various challenges and encounter dangerous creatures, but with their unwavering faith in their intuition, they emerge victorious. As they travel, they discover more artifacts and books that aid them in their quest. Despite the dangers they face, Tomas and his friends remain determined to protect others from the darkness and use their intuition to guide them on their journey.

Tomas and his friends, led by their intuition, continue to face dark and powerful entities. Despite banishing one entity, Tomas senses a greater darkness approaching. They encounter the enigmatic Wanderer, who offers Tomas a deal but disappears, leaving them in a twisted forest. They are then lured by Zara, who leads them into a trap. However, they are saved by an unknown force, and Tomas's mother appears. Though grateful, Tomas remains wary. Claire leads them through the forest, warning of being followed. As hooded figures close in, Tomas urges his friends to run.

In this thrilling and suspenseful story, Tomas and his friends find themselves in a dangerous situation as they face off against an ancient evil. With their intuition guiding them, they navigate through a series of challenges and encounters, including a stone altar, a dark book, and a battle with the Wanderer. Along the way, they discover the power of their friendship and the importance of relying on their instincts. As they investigate a mysterious massacre in the woods and explore an abandoned mansion, they encounter more supernatural forces and face the consequences of meddling in the affairs of the spirits. Despite the dangers they face, they remain determined and resilient, using their intuition to protect themselves and uncover the truth. As they continue their journey, they realize that they are being pursued and must stay vigilant. Through laughter and camaraderie, they find moments of joy amidst the darkness. However, their journey takes a dangerous turn when they are hit by another car and encounter three mysterious figures with glowing yellow eyes. The story ends on a cliffhanger, leaving readers eager to find out what happens next.

Tomas and his friends find themselves in a battle against evil forces that are after them. They encounter demon-like creatures, face off against an ancient evil in the Haunted Forest, and come across a mysterious figure in the town of Elmwood. As they navigate through these dangerous situations, they rely on their intuition and courage to survive. However, they soon discover that they have become subjects of an experiment conducted by scientists who want to harness the power of intuition. Doubting their own instincts, they must find a way to escape and defeat
the dark forces that are manipulating them.

Tomas and his friends find themselves drawn to a mysterious mansion, despite their intuition warning them to stay away. Inside, they discover a group of cloaked figures performing a ritual with an ornate box similar to one they had encountered before. The air is heavy with tension, and they can feel the dark energy emanating from the room. Tomas knows that they must confront the figures and stop whatever evil they are unleashing. With their intuition guiding them, they prepare for a battle against the darkness that threatens to consume them.

Tomas and his companions find themselves in a battle against dark forces that have been summoned into the world. They encounter cloaked figures, including Tomas' friend John, who has become a part of the supernatural. They fight for their lives, escaping the mansion and vowing to destroy the darkness. They continue their journey, facing battles with grotesque creatures and possessed individuals. They save a woman who turns out to be possessed, but ultimately banish the darkness with a powerful wave of light. They find themselves in a deserted town, where they encounter a woman named Sophia who offers to help them. With her guidance, they defeat more possessed beings and discover that the source of the darkness is a group of corrupted priests.

They banish the darkness and Sophia disappears, leaving Tomas with a sense of accomplishment and the realization that his intuition has
guided him to victory.

A horror novel

Chapter 1

Tomas had always been a man of integrity and intuition.

He trusted his gut, and it had never steered him wrong. So when his friend
John called him in a panic, he knew something was seriously wrong.
John was a skeptic, always dismissing Tomas's intuitive warnings as nonsense.
But now, he was begging for

Tomas's help, claiming there was a presence in his home.

Tomas raced to John's house, his heart pounding with a mix of fear and excitement. He had always been fascinated by the supernatural, but he had never experienced anything as intense as what was waiting for him inside John's front
door.
As soon as he stepped into the darkened foyer, Tomas felt it. The hairs on the
back of his neck stood up, and a chill
ran down his spine. The air was heavy and oppressive, and he could sense an almost palpable evil lurking in the shadows.

John was cowering in a corner, his eyes wide with terror.

Tomas tried to reassure him, but he could feel his own confidence slipping
away as the presence grew stronger.

Suddenly, something brushed past him in the darkness.

Tomas spun around, but there was nothing there. He could hear whispering,
faint and disembodied, coming from every corner of the room.

Then, as if on cue, the lights flickered and went out completely. Tomas was plunged into darkness, alone with the malevolent force that had taken over John's home.

He reached out a trembling hand, feeling his way along the wall. His heart was pounding in his chest, and he could feel sweat beading on his forehead.

Tomas knew he had to trust his intuition more than ever now. He had to find a way to fight back against the darkness, before it consumed them both.

Chapter 2

Despite the terrifying presence in John's home, Tomas refused to let fear consume him. With every ounce of
intuition he possessed, he scoured every inch of the house, determined to confront the entity and banish it once and for all.
As he moved through the darkened rooms, Tomas could feel his senses becoming sharper, more attuned to the world around him. He could sense the energy of the
malevolent force, feel its cold breath on the back of his neck, but he refused to let it overpower him.
With a steady hand, Tomas began to recite an incantation, calling upon the forces of light and goodness to banish the
darkness and restore balance to the world. At first, nothing happened, and Tomas gritted his teeth in frustration.
But then, something shifted. The malevolent presence seemed to pause, to hesitate, as if unsure of how to react.
Tomas seized upon this moment of uncertainty, channeling all of his intuition and strength into the incantation.
Slowly, imperceptibly, the darkness began to lift. The atmosphere in the house lightened, and the oppressive
aura of the malevolent entity retreated, becoming fainter and fainter until it was nothing but a distant memory.
As the light returned to the world once more, Tomas breathed a sigh of relief. He knew that the battle was far
from over, but he also knew that he possessed a powerful weapon in his intuition, a weapon that could help him

triumph over even the most malevolent of forces.

Chapter 3

Tomas left John's home feeling triumphant. His intuition had led him to the source of the malevolent presence, and he had banished it with ease. As he drove back to his own

A partment, Tomas couldn't help but feel a sense of unease. He had felt something during that confrontation, something he couldn't quite put his finger on.

He tried to shake off the feeling, telling himself that it was just residual fear from what he had just faced. But as the

night progressed, the feeling only grew stronger. It was a

nagging sensation, like someone was whispering in his ear. Tomas tried to push it away, but it only grew louder. Finally, he decided to investigate. He grabbed his flashlight and began to search his apartment, starting with the living room. He didn't have to search for long before he found something. There, in the corner of the room, was a small circle etched into the floor.

Tomas felt a chill run down his spine. He knew what it was. It was a summoning circle, a portal for dark entities to enter the mortal realm. Someone had been in his apartment, and they had been trying to summon something. Tomas didn't know who or what, but he knew that he needed to act fast.

He began to recite the same incantation that he had used in

John's home, hoping that it would be enough. But as he spoke, he felt the air grow colder, and the whispering in his ear grew louder. He could feel something watching him, something malevolent.

Tomas knew that he couldn't banish it alone. He needed help. He quickly grabbed his phone and dialed John's

number, hoping that he would answer. When John picked up, Tomas quickly explained the situation.

John didn't hesitate. He grabbed his things and rushed over to Tomas's apartment. When he arrived, Tomas led him to

the living room where the summoning circle still glowed faintly. Together, they recited the incantation, their voices growing louder and more confident with each passing moment.

Finally, with a burst of light, the summoning circle disappeared. The whispering in Tomas's ear ceased, and he felt the weight lift from his shoulders. The malevolent entity had been banished, just as before.

As John and Tomas sat in silence, catching their breath,

Tomas couldn't help but feel a sense of gratitude towards his friend. Without John's help, he would have been lost. As they sat, basking in the afterglow of their victory, they

knew that they couldn't let their guard down. The power of intuition was a gift, but it came with a price. They would always be on the lookout for the next threat, and they would be ready to face it head on.

Chapter 4

Tomas shuddered as he looked at the summoning circle etched onto his living room floor. How had he not noticed it before? He had always prided himself on his intuition, but now he felt like a fool. He had been living with this malevolent presence for God knows how long.

His mind immediately went to John. If there was one person he could trust with something like this, it was him. He dialed John's number and waited anxiously for him to answer.

"Hey, Tomas," John answered, sounding a bit groggy.

"John, I need your help again," Tomas said urgently. "I found a summoning circle in my apartment."

There was a moment of silence on the other end of the line before John spoke again. "I'll be there in ten minutes."

Tomas hung up the phone and walked back over to the circle. He had seen these before in books, but he had never expected to come across one in his own home. The candles that had once surrounded it had long since burned out, but he could still feel a residual energy emanating from the circle.

John arrived ten minutes later, looking just as tired as he had the night before. "Let's get to work," he said, already rolling up his sleeves.

Together, they began the same incantation that Tomas had used the night before. The words felt familiar on his tongue, but they were harder to say this time. The energy in the room was stronger, more oppressive.

Suddenly, something shifted in the air. The candles that had once burned out flickered to life once more, casting an eerie glow over the room. The energy in the room spiked, making Tomas feel like he was going to be sick.

And then, just as suddenly as it had begun, it was over. The candles flickered out once more and the energy in the room dissipated. Tomas felt like a weight had been lifted off his shoulders.

But he knew that this wasn't the end. There was still work to be done. He turned to John, his expression serious. "We need to find out who did this," he said. "We need to make sure they can't do it again."

Chapter 5

Tomas and John sat in silence, watching the flickering candles in the center of the summoning circle. They had expected a sudden rush of energy or an ominous presence to appear, but nothing had happened. It was as if the incantation had been a dud.

"Maybe we did something wrong," John said nervously.

Tomas shook his head. "I don't think so. I felt the energy shift. It's just...different than what I expected."

As they sat there, Tomas suddenly felt a sharp pain in his chest. He gasped and clutched at his heart, feeling like he was being squeezed in a vice.

"Are you okay?" John asked, reaching out to him.

Tomas shook his head, unable to speak for a moment.

Finally, he managed to gasp out, "It's not over. There's still something here."

John's eyes widened in fear as he realized what Tomas meant. They had only banished the entity from the

summoning circle, not from the apartment itself. It was still lurking somewhere, waiting for its chance to strike.

The two men leapt to their feet, grabbing candles and lighters as they searched the apartment frantically. They checked every room, every corner, every nook and cranny. But they found nothing.

It was only when they went back to the living room that they saw it. The summoning circle was still there, but now it glowed with an eerie red light. Slowly, the candles began to flicker out one by one, until there was only the red glow left.

Tomas and John looked at each other in horror. They had thought they were in control, that they could banish the

darkness with their intuition and strength. But now they

realized the truth. The power of intuition was just a drop in the ocean compared to the malevolent force they were facing.

And it was getting stronger. Chapter 6

Tomas fell to the ground, clutching his chest in agony. The pain was unbearable, and he could barely catch his breath. John panicked and began to recite the incantation they had used before, hoping it would work again. But this time, the entity was too powerful, and the incantation had no effect.

Suddenly, a bright light filled the room, and Tomas felt a force lifting him off the ground. He was levitating, surrounded by a white glow. The entity let out a deafening scream, and the candles on the summoning circle were blown out.

When the light dissipated, Tomas was on the ground, gasping for air, but the pain was gone. John helped him up, and they both looked around in amazement. The summoning circle was gone, and the room was back to normal.

They both knew something had happened, but they couldn't explain it. Tomas felt a strange energy coursing through him, and he knew that the entity was still out there, lurking in the shadows, waiting for its next victim.

A s they left the apartment, John turned to Tomas and said, "What the hell just happened in there?" Tomas didn't know how to answer. He had always believed in the power of intuition, but this was something else entirely.

Something unexpected had occurred, and he had no idea what it meant for their future.

But one thing was certain, they were not safe yet. The power of intuition had led them this far, but they were still in the grip of a malevolent entity, and they had to find a way to overcome it before it was too late.

Chapter 7

Tomas woke up in a cold sweat, the events of the night before haunting him. He could feel the presence of the malevolent entity lurking in the shadows, waiting to strike again. He knew he had to do something, but he didn't know what.

He spent the next few days pouring over books in the library, trying to find a solution to his problem. Finally, he

stumbled upon an ancient tome that promised to banish

even the most powerful of entities. The catch was that the ritual required a sacrifice, a life for a life. Tomas was hesitant, but he knew it was the only way to protect himself and those he loved. He called John and told him everything, hoping his friend would understand.

John arrived at Tomas's apartment, his face pale and scared. He knew the danger they were in, but he also knew that Tomas was a man of integrity and intuition, and he trusted him.

Together, they began the ritual. The candles flickered and the energy in the room spiked. Tomas could feel the entity's power growing stronger, but he didn't falter.

As they reached the final incantation, the room fell silent.

They both knew what needed to be done, but neither wanted to be the sacrifice.

Then, without warning, the entity spoke. Its voice was deep and menacing, and it promised to spare them in exchange for their allegiance.

Tomas and John exchanged a look, knowing what they had to do. They recited the final words of the ritual, sacrificing themselves to banish the entity once and for all.

As their bodies crumpled to the ground, the room erupted in a blinding light. When it faded, there was nothing left but the smell of burnt flesh and a single phrase etched into the wall:

"The power of intuition is nothing compared to the power of darkness."

Chapter 8

Days passed since Tomas and John's sacrifice, and the authorities had no leads on their disappearance. In the apartment complex, whispers of their strange behaviour before their disappearance spread like wildfire, and the police chalked it up to drugs or mental illness. But those who knew them knew better. They knew that something malevolent was at play.

One of Tomas's close friends, Alex, couldn't shake off the feeling that something was off. They had always trusted Tomas's intuition, and the fact that he and John disappeared right after a summoning ritual raised red flags.

Alex decided to investigate further and went to Tomas's apartment. As they entered the living room, they felt a chill run down their spine. The atmosphere was oppressive, and a strange energy filled the room.

Alex's intuition kicked in, and they knew they had to find a way to banish the entity. But they also knew that they couldn't do it alone.

They reached out to a psychic, Lila, who had a reputation

for dealing with supernatural entities. Lila was hesitant to get involved at first, but when she felt the energy in the room, she knew that this was no ordinary situation.

Together, they performed a ritual to banish the entity. As they chanted, the energy in the room intensified, and the candles flickered wildly. Suddenly, black smoke emerged from the floor, and a dark figure materialized in front of them.

Lila pushed Alex out of the way and faced the entity headon. From her pocket, she pulled out a golden talisman, and as she spoke the last words of the incantation, the talisman glowed with an otherworldly light.

The entity let out a blood-curdling scream and dissipated into the air. The energy in the room dissipated, and the candles flickered out.

Alex and Lila stood in silence, exhausted but relieved. As they made their way out of the apartment, Alex noticed a cryptic message etched on the wall, eerily familiar to the one that Tomas and John had left behind. Alex knew that they had to find out more. The malevolent entity was gone, but the mystery remained unsolved.

Chapter 9

As Alex and Lila stood in Tomas's apartment, trying to decipher the cryptic message on the wall, they heard a

knock on the door. Alex opened it to reveal a woman in her mid-twenties, her eyes wide with fear.

"I'm sorry to bother you," she said, "but I think there's something in my apartment. I don't know who else to turn to."

Alex and Lila exchanged a look, both knowing that they couldn't turn away someone in need. They followed the

woman down the hall to her apartment, which was filled with a heavy, oppressive energy.

As they walked through the rooms, Alex could feel the hairs on the back of her neck standing up. She knew that they

were dealing with something powerful and malevolent. But as they neared the woman's bedroom, Lila suddenly stopped in her tracks.

"Wait," she said, her eyes closed in concentration. "I sense something else here. Something....familiar."

Alex looked at her, confused. "What do you mean?"

Lila opened her eyes and turned to her. "I think we've dealt with this entity before. In Tomas's apartment."

Alex felt a chill run down her spine. "Are you saying that

Tomas and John didn't banish it? That it's still out there, feeding on innocent people?"

Lila nodded gravely. "I think that's exactly what I'm saying."

19

As they continued their investigation, Alex and Lila couldn't shake the feeling that they were being watched.

And when they finally found the source of the malevolent presence, they knew that they were in for a fight. A fight that they might not win.

But they also knew that they couldn't back down. Not when there were innocent lives at stake.

They took a deep breath and prepared for battle.

Chapter 10

Alex and Lila stood outside the woman's apartment, their hearts racing with fear. They knew what they were about to face: a powerful and malevolent entity that had already

Taken the lives of Tomas and John. But they had no choice. Innocent lives were at stake, and they were the only ones with the power to stop it.

They took a deep breath and knocked on the door. A young woman answered. She had dark circles under her eyes and a haunted look in her gaze. "Please, come in," she said. "I

don't know what's happening to me. I hear voices, and I see things. Terrible things."

Alex and Lila exchanged a worried glance. They had heard this story before. It was the same entity that Tomas and John had faced, and it seemed to be growing stronger with each passing day.

They followed the woman into her living room, where they saw the telltale signs of an entity's presence: objects moving on their own, whispers in the air, a sudden drop in temperature.

Without a word, Alex and Lila pulled out their tools and began setting up their defenses. They sprinkled salt around the perimeter of the room, lit candles, and chanted incantations to create a protective barrier.

But they knew it wouldn't be enough. This entity was too powerful, too cunning, too determined.

As they worked, they heard the woman's cries growing louder. "Please, make it stop! Make it go away!"

But they couldn't. They were no match for this entity. They were only buying time, hoping to find a way to banish it permanently before it was too late.

Suddenly, they heard a noise coming from the bedroom.

Lila crept towards the door, her heart pounding in her chest. She pushed it open and saw someone standing in the shadows.

It was a man, tall and lean, with a stern look on his face. "Who are you?" Lila asked, her hand on her weapon.

"I'm here to help," he said, his voice low and steady.

Alex and Lila exchanged a wary glance. They had been burned before, trusting strangers who claimed to be able to help. But something about this man's energy felt different. Stronger. More sincere.

They nodded in silence, and the man stepped forward, his hands outstretched.

He began chanting an incantation, his voice rising in power and intensity.

For a moment, nothing happened. The room was still, the air thick with tension.

And then, suddenly, the entity appeared, its form coalescing out of thin air. It was a grotesque, twisted thing, with eyes that glowed red and sharp claws that dripped with blood.

But the man didn't back down. He kept chanting, his voice growing louder and more forceful. And slowly, the entity began to weaken. Its form flickered and wavered, its power draining away.

And then, with a final burst of energy, it vanished, leaving behind only the scent of sulfur and a sense of relief.

Alex and Lila looked at each other, stunned. They had never seen anything like it. The man turned to them, a small smile on his lips. "My name is Michael," he said. "And I think we have a lot to talk about."

Chapter 11

Alex and Lila sat in Michael's car, trying to process what had just happened. The entity had been banished, but the aftermath left them shaken.

"Who are you?" Lila finally asked Michael, breaking the silence.

"I'm just a guy who knows a thing or two about the supernatural," Michael replied cryptically. "And I knew you two needed help."

"Why did Tomas and John sacrifice themselves?" Alex asked, still trying to understand the message they left behind.

Michael sighed and looked out the window. "Tomas and

John were good men. They knew what they had to do to banish the entity. Sometimes sacrifices have to be made to protect others."

"But what does the message mean?" Lila pressed.

Michael turned to them, his eyes somber. "It means that the darkness is still out there. It means that there are

Forces beyond our understanding that we can't control. But it also means that there are people, like you and me, who are willing to fight back against it."

Alex and Lila nodded in agreement. They had seen the power of the supernatural firsthand, and they knew that they had to be prepared for anything.

As Michael dropped them off back at their apartment, he handed them each a small silver amulet. "This will help protect you from evil spirits. It's not foolproof, but it

should buy you some time if you're ever caught off guard."

"Thank you," Lila said, tucking the amulet into her pocket.

Michael gave them a small smile. "You two have potential. Keep fighting the good fight."

With that, he drove off into the night, leaving Alex and Lila feeling both grateful and confused.

"We have to keep investigating," Alex said determinedly as they walked into their apartment.

Lila nodded in agreement. "We can't let Tomas and John's sacrifice be in vain."

They sat down at their computer, ready to dive back into researching the supernatural. They knew that the darkness was out there, but they were ready to use their intuition and fight back against it.

Chapter 12

Alex and Lila had decided to take a break from investigating after the intense encounter with the malevolent entity. They spent the day browsing a local bookstore, hoping to distract themselves from the horrors they had witnessed. As they perused the shelves, Alex's

E yes darted to a spine marked with a rust-colored symbol. He walked over and pulled the book from the shelf, flipping through the pages until he found the section he was looking for.

"What is it?" Lila asked, sensing a change in Alex's demeanor. "Look at this," he said, pointing to a passage about ancient symbols used to banish evil spirits. "Tomas mentioned something similar before he disappeared."

Lila nodded thoughtfully. "Maybe we should see if Michael knows anything about this."

Determined to find answers, they made their way to the address Michael had left them. As they approached the

door, they heard chanting from inside. They exchanged a

nervous glance before knocking. When Michael opened the door, he was in the midst of a ritual with two other individuals. He welcomed Alex and Lila in and invited them to join the ceremony.

As they participated in the ritual, the room began to vibrate with energy. Alex and Lila felt like they were floating, enveloped in a powerful force. Suddenly, Michael opened his eyes and looked directly at them.

"Your intuition is strong," he said. "But it can also be dangerous. Trust it, but be cautious. The spirits are always watching."

Alex and Lila nodded, feeling a sense of urgency. They thanked Michael for his guidance and left.

As they walked back to their car, Lila spoke up. "Do you think Tomas and John were involved in this kind of thing?"

"It's possible," Alex said. "But we don't know enough yet. We need to keep digging."

They got in the car and drove off into the night, determined to uncover the truth behind Tomas and John's disappearance and the malevolent entities that seemed to be haunting them.

Chapter 13

The next day, Alex and Lila decided to take a break from investigating and went on a date to a local amusement
park. They rode roller coasters, ate cotton candy, and
enjoyed the summer

sun. For a moment, they forgot about the darkness that
they had faced, and embraced the joy that life could offer.

As they walked through the park, Alex suddenly stopped in his tracks. He felt
a strange sensation in the pit of his
stomach, like something was off. Lila noticed his change in demeanor and
asked if he was okay.

"I don't know," Alex said. "I just have this feeling, like we're being watched."
Lila nodded, taking Michael's warning to heart. She looked around, but every-thing seemed normal. However, as they walked through the park, the feeling persisted. They
Decided to call it a day and headed back to their apartment.
As they walked into the building, they noticed an unfamiliar woman
standing in the lobby, her eyes fixed on them. She was wearing a long flowing
skirt and a shawl that covered most of her face.
Alex and Lila exchanged a look, and then approached the woman cautiously.
The woman turned towards them and removed her shawl. It was Michael's as-sistant, Sophie.
"I'm sorry to startle you," Sophie said. "I just wanted to give you this."
She handed them a small box with a note attached. The note read, "Follow
your intuition, and don't forget the power of love and light."

Alex and Lila thanked Sophie, feeling reassured by her presence. As they walked to their apartment, they opened the box to find two amulets, just like the one Michael had given them before.

They put them on, feeling a sense of protection wash over them. They sat on the couch, enjoying each other's company and feeling

grateful for the light that they had found in each other.

But as the sun set and darkness fell, they couldn't shake the feeling that they were being watched. They listened carefully, their intuition on high alert. The spirits were always watching, and they had to be ready for whatever came next.

Chapter 14

Despite their apprehension, Alex and Lila decided to take a break from the supernatural investigations and spend a
day at the beach. The warm sun and the sound of the waves crashing onto the shore made them forget about the
horrors they had encountered in the past weeks.
As they lounged on the sand, Alex couldn't help but notice how relaxed Lila looked, almost as if she had left all her worries behind. He smiled to himself, grateful for this moment of respite.
They went for a swim in the clear blue water, feeling the coolness wash away their stress. For a moment, they forgot about the amulets and the threats they had faced, and
simply enjoyed the simple pleasure of swimming.
As the sun began to set, they sat on the beach, watching the orange glow of the horizon. Lila leaned her head on Alex's shoulder, feeling content.
"We needed this," she said softly. "To remember that there's still beauty in the world."
Alex nodded, feeling the same way. "I'm glad we took a break. It's good for us to recharge."
They sat in comfortable silence, listening to the sound of the waves and the occasional seagull. For a moment, everything felt
light and easy, as if the weight of the world had lifted off their shoulders.
But as the night fell, they had to face the reality of their situation. The amulets may offer some protection, but they were not invincible. The spirits were always watching and waiting for their next move.

As they made their way back home, Alex and Lila felt a sense of unease creeping back into their minds. But they

knew they had to continue their investigation, to fight back against the darkness that threatened to take over their lives.

They held hands, drawing strength from each other, as they prepared for what lay ahead. They would trust their

intuition, just as Michael had advised, and fight back with all their might. The power of the supernatural may be overwhelming, but the power of their determination was stronger still.

Chapter 15

As the sun set and darkness descended upon the city, Alex and Lila found themselves walking down a deserted street.

The only sounds were the chirping of crickets and the distant hum of traffic. Though they felt protected by the amulets, they still couldn't shake off the feeling of unease that had been haunting them for days. Suddenly, Lila grabbed Alex's arm, causing him to jump.

"What is it?" he asked, scanning the street.

"I don't know... I just feel like we're being watched," Lila said.

Alex turned to her and saw the fear in her eyes. He squeezed her hand, trying to comfort her.

"It's okay. We have the amulets. Nothing can hurt us," he said, more to reassure himself than Lila.

Suddenly, they both heard a rustling sound coming from an alleyway up ahead. Their hearts racing, they cautiously approached the alleyway. They couldn't see anything in the darkness, but they could feel a malevolent presence nearby.

Suddenly, a pair of glowing eyes appeared in the darkness. Lila screamed and stumbled back, but Alex stood his ground. He pulled out a small flashlight and shone it in the direction of the eyes. A shadowy figure emerged from the darkness, its eyes blazing with a demonic energy.

Alex and Lila backed away, but the figure didn't move. It just stood there, watching them with its glowing eyes. Suddenly, Tomas appeared from behind the figure and grabbed it by the shoulder. The figure let out a piercing scream and dissolved into a cloud of dark mist.

"Are you guys okay?" Tomas asked, looking at Alex and Lila.

They nodded, still shaken from the encounter.

"What was that thing?" Lila asked, her voice trembling.

"I don't know for sure, but I have a feeling it's not the last we'll see of it," Tomas replied, his intuition burning bright.
As they walked away from the alleyway, they knew that their fight against the darkness was far from over. But they also knew that they had each other and the power of their intuition to guide them through the darkness.

Chapter 16

Tomas led Alex and Lila to a nearby diner, his eyes scanning the streets for any sign of the shadowy figure. As

they ordered coffee and pie, Tomas eased into lighthearted conversation, his wit and charm putting the couple at ease. They forgot their worries, at least for a moment, as they talked about their childhoods and shared humorous stories.

It was a refreshing break from the darkness that had engulfed their lives, and Alex and Lila found themselves laughing and

smiling in a way they hadn't in a long time. For that brief moment, they felt normal.

But the feeling didn't last long.

As they left the diner and made their way back to Alex's apartment, they noticed the streets were emptier than

usual. A sense of unease crept over them once more, and they quickened their pace.

It was then that they saw him. The shadowy figure loomed in the distance, its glowing eyes fixed upon them.

Without hesitation, Tomas stepped forward, his intuition guiding him. The amulet around his neck glowed with a

bright light, and the shadowy figure recoiled, letting out a hiss before disappearing into the darkness.

Breathless and shaken, the trio continued on their way, their pace quickened once more. They knew their fight against the darkness was far from over, but for that moment, they were grateful to have each other.

As they reached Alex's apartment, Tomas bid them farewell, promising to stay in touch. Alex and Lila watched him disappear into the night, a sense of gratitude washing over them.

Perhaps they couldn't banish the darkness completely, but with Tomas by their side, they felt a glimmer of hope. And

with that hope, they knew they could continue the fight, no matter how daunting the task might seem.

Chapter 17

As they walked back to their hotel, Alex, Lila, and Tomas stay alert, scanning their surroundings for any signs of the shadowy figure that had followed them. The street was eerily quiet, with no cars or people in sight. The only sound was the sound of their footsteps echoing against the pavement.

Suddenly, they hear a shrill scream coming from an alleyway a few feet ahead. They rushed to the source of the noise and found a woman lying on the ground, her clothes torn and her body covered in bruises. She looked up at them with terror in her eyes as she muttered, "it was him, he's coming."

Before they could react, a figure emerged from the shadows, tall and menacing. Its eyes glowed red, and it let out a guttural growl, causing the woman to scream again and cover her face. Alex, Lila, and Tomas stood frozen, unsure of what to do.

The figure charged at them, and Alex and Lila instinctively reached for their amulets. The figure was thrown back by some invisible force, and it let out a roar of frustration as it vanished into thin air.

The woman sat up, visibly shaking, and thanked them for saving her. She explained that she had seen the same figure stalking her for days, and she knew it was only a matter of time before it attacked. She begged them to help her, but before they could respond, the figure reappeared in a cloud of smoke.

This time, it was not alone. Dozens of shadowy figures materialized around them, their eyes glowing with malevolence. The woman let out a blood-curdling scream as they advanced on her.

Alex, Lila, and Tomas stood back to back, their amulets glowing with a fierce white light. They could feel the power
of their intuition surging through them, but they knew that they were vastly outnumbered. They braced themselves for the fight of their lives.

Chapter 18

As the shadowy figures closed in on them, Alex, Lila, and

Tomas held their amulets tightly and chanted the words that had become second nature to them. The power of their
combined energy
formed a protective bubble around them, repelling the dark entities. The trio continued walking, making sure to stay close together.
Tomas felt a knot form in his stomach, a feeling he had learned to trust. Something wasn't right. He scanned the
area and noticed a man lurking in the shadows, watching them intently. Tomas suddenly had a vision of the man's face contorted in anger, and he knew that he couldn't be trusted.
He immediately alerted Alex and Lila, and they picked up their pace, but the man began following them, his
breathing heavy as he gained on them. They turned a
corner and found themselves in a dead-end alleyway.
The man emerged from the shadows, revealing his true form—the malevolent presence that had been haunting
John's house. Alex, Lila, and Tomas stood their ground, knowing that they had no other choice but to face the entity head-on.
The malevolent presence let out a bone-chilling laugh and lunged at them. They used their amulets to fend off the

entity's attacks, but it was no match for their combined

power. The entity screeched and vanished, leaving behind a trail of smoke as it dissipated into the night.

Tomas felt a sense of relief wash over him, grateful that they had triumphed over their latest foe. But he knew that their work was far from over, and there were still dark forces lurking in the shadows, waiting to strike.

As they made their way back to their hotel, Tomas couldn't shake the feeling that there was something different about the darkness they were fighting. It was stronger, more malevolent than anything they had faced before. Tomas knew that they had to be prepared for what was to come, because their intuition was telling them that the worst was yet to come.

Chapter 19

Despite their success in defeating the malevolent presence, Alex, Lila, and Tomas couldn't shake off the feeling of dread that came with the encounter. They knew that they had to be more vigilant than ever before, and they spent the next few days preparing themselves for any possible attacks.

Tomas, in particular, was more focused and driven than ever before. He spent hours poring over ancient texts and scrolls, trying to find any clues that could help them in their fight against the darkness.

One night, as they sat in their hotel room, a sudden knock on the door interrupted their research. Tomas's intuition told him that something was wrong, and he promptly grabbed his amulet before answering the door.

To their surprise, they found John standing outside, looking pale and disheveled. He stumbled into the room, muttering about how he had been pursued by dark entities for days. He told them how he had discovered a strange book in his attic, which he had foolishly opened, unleashing a malevolent force that had been haunting him ever since.

Tomas listened intently, his intuition telling him that John's story was more than just a coincidence. He knew that there was something about this book that was intimately tied to their mission, and he made up his mind to find out what it was.

The next day, they set out to John's house, determined to investigate the strange book for themselves. As they reached the attic, they found the book lying on a pedestal, its pages filled with incomprehensible symbols and sigils.

Tomas felt a surge of power emanating from the book, and he knew that it was a powerful artifact that could either aid them or destroy them. He hesitated for a moment, wondering whether to take the book with them or leave it be.

But his intuition told him that this was a risk worth taking.

He held out his hand and grabbed the book, feeling a rush of power surging through his veins.

Little did he know, the book would unlock a series of events that would change their lives forever.

Chapter 20

The artifact drew them in like a magnet, and they couldn't tear their eyes away from it. Its ancient design was intricate and mesmerizing, and they knew instinctively that it was imbued with power beyond their wildest imagination.

But there was something else, too. A feeling that they couldn't quite place, but that made their skin crawl. It was

As if the artifact was alive, pulsing with malevolent energy. Tomas was the first to snap out of the trance, and he turned to look at the others. "We need to take this thing and get out of here," he said, his voice low and urgent.

Alex and Lila nodded, and they carefully wrapped the artifact in a cloth before making their way to the door.

As they stepped out into the hallway, they were startled by the sound of someone clearing their throat. They turned to see a tall, slender man standing at the end of the corridor, watching them with a curious expression.

"Can I help you?" Tomas asked, his hand already reaching for his amulet.

The man smiled, revealing perfectly white teeth. "I think you might be able to help me," he said. "My name is Adam, and I've been following your progress for some time now." The three of them exchanged wary glances. "How do you know about us?" Lila asked.

Adam shrugged. "Let's just say that I have my sources. But that's not important right now. What is important is that we work together."

Tomas narrowed his eyes. "Why should we trust you?"

"Because I know things," Adam replied cryptically.

"Things that could help you in your fight against the darkness. But we don't have much time. The artifact you're

holding is drawing attention. You need to come with me, now."

There was a sense of urgency in his voice that they couldn't ignore. With a nod, they followed Adam down the hallway and into an elevator.

As the doors closed, Tomas couldn't shake the feeling that they were stepping into something far more dangerous

than anything they had faced before. But he also knew that they had no choice but to trust Adam, at least for now.

The elevator doors opened again, and they stepped out into a dimly lit room. In the center of the room was a table, and on the table was a map.

Adam gestured to the map. "This is where we need to go," he said. "The artifact you're holding is just the beginning.

There's so much more out there, buried in the darkness.

And we need to find it before it's too late."

Chapter 21

Determined to uncover more artifacts, the trio set off on their quest, following the map that Adam had given them. They trekked through

dense forests and barren wastelands, treading carefully

and keeping their senses alert for any signs of danger.
As the sun began to set, they came across a small, abandoned town. The buildings were dilapidated and the streets were eerily quiet. Despite their apprehension, they decided to

search for clues that might lead them to the next artifact.

Tomas's intuition led him towards an old, rundown house on the outskirts of the town. As they approached the house, they heard strange noises coming from inside. They
cautiously entered, each holding their amulets tightly.
The interior of the house was in shambles, with broken furniture and cobwebs covering every surface. But as they made their way through the house, they felt an overwhelming energy permeating the air.
Suddenly, the floor beneath them began to shake and crack. The walls shuddered, and they heard a deafening roar that shook the very foundations of the house.
Out of nowhere, a massive, dark entity emerged from the shadows, its glowing eyes filled with malice. It towered over them, its twisted limbs and sharp claws surrounding them.

But something unexpected happened. The entity did not attack them. Instead, it bowed its head and spoke in a voice that sounded like a thousand screams. "You have come seeking power," it said. "But you do not know what it is you seek. Beware, for there are forces beyond your comprehension at work here." And with that, the entity vanished into thin air, leaving the trio shaken and confused.

As they made their way out of the house, they knew that their mission had just become even more dangerous and that they

needed to be prepared for whatever lay ahead. Chapter 22

Tomas, Alex, and Lila stumbled out of the abandoned town, shaken by their encounter with the dark entity. They were relieved to be in the safety of their car, but their relief was short-lived when the engine refused to start.

As they pondered their next move, a figure emerged from the shadows. It was a young woman, no more than twenty, with pale skin and long dark hair. She wore a tattered wool coat and clutched a small leather-bound book.

"Are you lost?" she asked, watching them with unwavering intensity.

Tomas hesitated before answering. He sensed something familiar about her, something that made his intuition hum. "We're looking for something," he said carefully.

The woman cocked her head, her dark eyes gleaming. "I know what you're looking for," she said softly. "I can help you find it."

Alex and Lila exchanged a meaningful glance, but Tomas seemed to be in a trance. "Who are you?" he asked the woman.

She smiled wryly. "I go by many names. Let's just say I'm a friend."

Tomas felt his skepticism slipping away. There was something about this woman that made him trust her, despite all his training and his better judgment. "Lead the way," he said, and the woman stepped forward, beckoning them into the night.

As they followed her deeper into the abandoned town, Tomas felt a sense of unease creeping over him. He couldn't quite put his finger on it, but he knew that they were in danger. Nevertheless, the woman led them to a crumbling building on the outskirts of town.

She led them down a creaking stairway and into a basement room filled with dust and shadows. There, in the center of the room, was an ornate box.

Tomas approached it cautiously, aware of the dark energy emanating from it. The woman spoke softly at his side.

"That is what you seek. Take it, and use it well."

Tomas hesitated, but Lila and Alex were already handling the box, examining its intricate carvings and gilded edges. "We need this," Alex said firmly. "We need to stop the darkness."

Tomas nodded, and the woman smiled again. "Good luck," she said, and she vanished into the shadows.

As they left the town behind, Tomas felt something stirring inside of him. He knew that their journey was far from

over, but for the first time, he felt a glimmer of hope. The

young woman had given him a sense of peace, a sense that they were not alone in their fight against the darkness.

They would continue on, together, and perhaps they would prevail.

Chapter 23

As they walked through the woods, Alex, Lila, and Tomas couldn't shake off the feeling of being watched. They had left the abandoned town with the ornate box, but the weight of their mission seemed to grow heavier with each step they took. Suddenly, they heard a rustling in the bushes and turned around, ready for whatever may come their way.

To their surprise, they saw a young man emerging from the foliage, dressed in a tattered and torn black cloak. His long hair was unkempt and his eyes were piercing blue, staring at them with a mixture of curiosity and suspicion.

"Who are you?" Tomas asked, his intuition telling him to be cautious.

The young man smirked. "I could ask you the same thing. What brings you three here?"

"We're searching for artifacts," Alex said bluntly, not wanting to waste any time. "To stop the darkness that's been plaguing us."

The young man's expression softened slightly. "I see. I've been on a similar quest myself. My name is Marcus. Perhaps we could help each other out?"

Tomas studied Marcus carefully, his intuition telling him that the young man was trustworthy. "What do you know about the artifacts?" he asked.

Marcus pulled out a small, leather-bound book from his cloak and flipped through the pages. "I've been traveling for months, studying ancient texts and searching for clues. I believe I have information that could be of use to you."

As Marcus read from the book, Alex, Lila, and Tomas listened intently, their minds racing with possibilities. It was clear that Marcus was a valuable addition to their team, and they couldn't help but feel a glimmer of hope.

But even as they continued on their journey, they couldn't shake off the feeling that there was something dark and ominous looming in the shadows, waiting for them to make a wrong move. They had no choice but to press onward, their intuition telling them that the stakes were too high to turn back now.

Chapter 24

Tomas, Alex, Lila, and Marcus trudged through the dense woods, following Marcus's lead towards the next artifact. The air was thick with an oppressive energy, and Tomas couldn't shake the feeling that they were being watched. As they pushed deeper into the woods, the trees began to thin out until they reached a clearing. In the center of the clearing stood a small cabin, its windows boarded up and its paint peeling.

Marcus hesitated, his eyes flickering over the run-down cabin. "This is the place," he said, his voice low. "But we need to be careful."

The group approached the cabin slowly, their senses on high alert. As they drew closer, they could see that the door was slightly ajar.

Tomas held his breath and cautiously pushed the door open, revealing a small, cramped interior. The air was thick with dust, and the floorboards creaked under their feet.

Suddenly, a dark, swirling mist began to fill the room, causing the group to cough and gag. Gasping for air, they reached for their amulets, hoping to protect themselves from the darkness.

But no matter how hard they tried, the dark mist continued to swirl around them, choking them with its oppressive energy.

Just when they thought they couldn't take it anymore, the mist suddenly dissipated as quickly as it had appeared, leaving the group gasping for air.

As they caught their breath, they noticed something strange on the floor. It was an ornate key, made of what looked like antique silver.

Without hesitation, they scooped up the key and continued their search for the next artifact, their hearts pounding with excitement and fear. They knew that the darkness was closing in on them, and time was running out.

Chapter 25

As they walked deeper into the woods, the four friends could feel the tension growing. The ornate key they had
found in the cabin seemed to be leading them somewhere, but they didn't know where. Suddenly, a voice echoed in their minds.

"Stop. There is danger ahead."

It was Tomas's intuition speaking to them again, warning them of the unknown dangers that lay ahead of them.

"We have to keep going," Lila said, determined to find the next artifact.

They followed the key's direction until they came across a clearing in the woods. In the center of the clearing was a stone altar with a glowing purple crystal on top of it. "We've found it," Marcus said, his voice shaking with excitement.

But as they approached the altar, they could feel the energy shift around them. The air grew thick, and the temperature dropped. Suddenly, they were surrounded by a group of figures in dark cloaks.

"Who are you?" Alex demanded, his hand clutching the amulet around his neck.

"We are the keepers of the crystal," one of the figures replied, his voice cold and menacing. "And you are not welcome here."

Without warning, the figures attacked. It was a blur of movement as the friends fought back, using every weapon and spell at their disposal. Tomas's intuition allowed him to sense the attacks before they happened, giving him an advantage over the supernatural foes.

Just when it seemed like the fight was lost, the crystal on the altar shattered, and the figures disappeared into the ether.

Breathing heavily, the friends looked around the clearing, unsure of what had just happened.

"We did it," Lila said, a look of triumph on her face.

But as they turned to leave, they could feel the dark energy swirling around them, threatening to consume them.

"We have to hurry," Tomas said, his intuition screaming at him to move quickly. "We have to get these artifacts together before it's too late."

The four friends raced out of the woods, the weight of their mission heavy on their shoulders. They knew that the darkness was growing stronger, and they were the only ones who could stop it.

Chapter 26

Tomas felt uneasy as they continued their journey, their next destination unknown. The attack in the cabin had
shaken him, and he couldn't shake off the feeling that they were being watched. Alex, Lila, and Marcus didn't seem to share his apprehension, but Tomas knew better than to ignore his intuition.
As they walked deeper into the woods, the trees grew thicker, and the air grew colder. The silence was
oppressive, broken only by their footsteps and the
occasional rustling of leaves. Tomas took the lead, his eyes scanning the area for any signs of danger.
Suddenly, he spotted movement in the bushes up ahead. He held up a hand, signaling the others to stop. They froze, watching as a figure emerged from the foliage. It was a
man, tall and lean, with piercing blue eyes and a jagged scar running down one cheek.
"Who are you?" Tomas asked, his hand on the hilt of his sword.
The man grinned, revealing a row of sharp teeth. "I'm the one you've been looking for," he said. "I have what you seek."
Tomas felt a surge of suspicion. "What do you want in return?" he asked.
The man's grin widened. "A life for a life," he said. "You take my place, and I'll give you what you want."
Tomas hesitated. The man's offer seemed too good to be true, and the price was steep. But he knew that they couldn't afford to waste any more time.
"Deal," he said, and stepped forward to take the man's place.

As soon as he did, the man vanished, replaced by a shimmering portal. Tomas took a deep breath, then
stepped through the portal, hoping that his intuition had led him down the right path.

Chapter 27

Tomas found himself in a dimly lit room, surrounded by stacks of dusty books and ancient artifacts. The man who had led him through the portal stood in front of him, a sly grin on his face.

"Well, well, well. Tomas, the man of intuition, finally made it to the other side," the man said, his voice dripping with sarcasm.

Tomas ignored him and scanned the room. He saw a book on a pedestal that glowed with a faint, purple light. He knew that was what he had come for.

"You want this?" the man asked, holding up the book. Tomas nodded, his heart racing.

"Then you know what you have to do," the man said, his grin widening.

Tomas hesitated. He knew what the man wanted, but he didn't want to sacrifice anyone else's life. He couldn't live with that guilt.

Suddenly, he felt a hand on his shoulder. He turned and saw Alex, Lila, and Marcus standing behind him.

"We're with you, Tomas," Alex said, a determined look on his face.

Tomas felt a surge of gratitude and determination. He wouldn't have to do this alone.

He turned to the man and said, "I'll take the book, but I won't sacrifice anyone else's life. I'm willing to make the sacrifice myself."

The man's grin disappeared, replaced by a look of surprise and admiration.

"Very well," he said, handing the book to Tomas.

As soon as Tomas touched the book, he felt a surge of power flow through his body. He knew that this was the key to stopping the darkness.

The group made their way back to the cabin where they had found the first artifact. They placed the book on the altar and watched as it glowed with a bright, purple light.

Suddenly, the air around them grew colder and a gust of wind blew through the cabin. The darkness was getting stronger.

Tomas knew what they had to do. They had to find the last artifact and combine it with the other two to banish the darkness once and for all.

But he also knew that the darkness would do whatever it could to stop them. They had to be ready for anything.

With a sense of purpose and determination, Tomas and his friends set out into the woods, ready to face whatever lay ahead.

Chapter 28

As they made their way deeper into the woods, Tomas couldn't
shake the feeling that they were being watched. He kept his hand on the hilt of
his sword, ready for any attackers. Alex, Lila, and Marcus were on edge too.
They knew they were close to finding the last artifact, but they also knew they
were running out of time.
Suddenly, they heard a rustling in the bushes. Tomas raised his sword, ready to
strike, but instead of a monster,
a figure emerged from the foliage. It was a woman, wearing a long, flowing
dress that looked like it had been there for centuries. She had a wild look in
her eyes and a necklace made of bones around her neck.
Tomas stepped forward. "Who are you?" he asked.
The woman cackled. "I am the protector of the final artifact," she said. "And
you will never get it from me." Tomas didn't know how to respond. He had
come too far to be stopped now. "What do you want?" he asked.
"I want your blood," the woman said, lunging at him with a knife.
Tomas dodged her attack and swung his sword, barely missing her face. She
screeched and leapt back, disappearing into the woods.
The four friends continued on, following the trail the woman had left behind.
Eventually, they came to a
clearing, where a stone pillar stood tall in the center. Tomas felt a chill go
down his spine. He knew that the final artifact was here.
As they approached the stone pillar, a figure emerged from the shadows. It was
Michael, the man who had sent them
on this quest in the first place. "You've found it," he said, a smile spreading
across his face.

Tomas narrowed his eyes. "What is this all about?" he demanded. Michael's smile faded. "You don't understand,"
he said. "This is
bigger than any of us. The darkness is growing, and we need to stop it before it's too late."
Tomas still didn't trust him, but he knew they had come too far to turn back now. He reached out and grasped the
final artifact, a glowing crystal, in his hand. Suddenly, the ground shook beneath their feet, and the sky turned dark. The darkness had reached them.

Chapter 29

Tomas and his friends stood in front of Michael, staring at him in disbelief. "What do you mean, we need to stop the darkness? We already defeated it," Tomas said.

Michael sighed. "You only defeated a small part of it. The darkness is still growing, and it's getting stronger every day. You need to find a way to banish it for good."

"But how?" Lila asked.

"There's only one way," Michael replied. "You need to destroy the source of the darkness. And that source is...you, Tomas."

Tomas stepped back in shock. "What are you talking about? How can I be the source of the darkness?"

"When you made the deal with the man in the woods, you opened a door to a realm of darkness and allowed it to enter our world. And now, it's growing stronger because of you," Michael explained.

Tomas felt a wave of guilt wash over him. "I had no idea. How can I fix this?"

"You need to sacrifice yourself," Michael said.

Tomas looked at his friends, his heart heavy. "I don't know if I can do that."

"You have to," Michael said firmly. "The fate of the world depends on it."

Tomas took a deep breath and nodded. "Okay. Let's do it." His friends protested, but he was resolute. Together, they prepared for the ritual that would banish the darkness once and for all. Tomas stood in the middle of the circle, holding the amulet that Michael had given him.

As the ritual began, Tomas felt a surge of power coursing through him. He closed his eyes and focused on the task at hand, embracing the darkness and turning it against itself.

It was a painful process, but he kept going, knowing that it was the only way to save the world.

Finally, he felt a surge of energy rip through him, and he collapsed onto the ground. When he opened his eyes, he saw that the darkness was gone, replaced by a bright light. His friends rushed to his side, helping him up.

"You did it," Michael said, a hint of pride in his voice. Tomas smiled weakly. "We did it."

They hugged each other tightly, grateful to be alive and free from the darkness. But they knew that it was only a matter of time before another threat appeared. They would be ready for it, though, armed with the power of intuition and their unbreakable bond of friendship.

Chapter 30

Tomas woke up to the sound of his friends talking. He was lying on a soft bed, surrounded by unfamiliar objects. As he
sat up, he felt a
sharp pain in his chest, causing him to gasp. Alex noticed Tomas' discomfort and walked towards him.

"Tomas, are you okay?" Alex asked, looking concerned.

Tomas nodded, trying to regain his composure. "Yeah, I'm alright. What happened? Where are we?"

Lila spoke next, "We're at Michael's. You passed out after the ritual."

Tomas looked around and saw that they were in a small room that resembled a library. The shelves were filled with books on magic and the occult, and there was a large wooden desk in the center of the room.

"Michael said that the darkness is gone," Alex said, a smile on his face.

Tomas felt a wave of relief wash over him, but he couldn't shake the feeling that something was off. He got out of bed and walked towards the window, looking outside. The sun was setting, casting an orange glow over the landscape.

Tomas saw that they were in a deserted area, surrounded by tall trees and overgrown bushes.

"How long have I been asleep?" Tomas asked, turning to face his friends.

"Almost a day," Lila replied, "We've been taking turns watching over you."

Tomas rubbed his eyes, feeling a headache coming on. He suddenly remembered Michael's words about destroying the source of the darkness.

"Hey, guys... Michael said that the source of the darkness was me. What did he mean?" Tomas asked, looking at his friends.

Alex and Lila exchanged a look, unsure of how to explain it to Tomas.

"Michael said that the darkness was connected to your family, Tomas. We don't know how, but he thinks that you might have some kind of power that can control it," Alex said, his voice hesitant.

Tomas felt a chill run down his spine as he realized that everything that had happened was connected to him. He felt a sudden urge to run away, to hide from the truth.

"Do you think that's possible? That I have some kind of power?" Tomas asked, his voice trembling.

Lila placed a hand on Tomas' shoulder, "Anything is possible, Tomas. Especially after what we've been through. But whatever happens, we'll face it together."

Tomas felt a surge of gratitude and determination, knowing that he had his friends by his side.

"Okay. Let's figure this out," Tomas said, determination in his voice.

As they sat down to discuss their next steps, Tomas felt a strange sensation in his chest, as if something was awakening inside him. He felt a surge of power, and he Knew that this was just the beginning. The darkness might have been banished, but there was no telling what other horrors awaited them. Tomas was ready to face them head-on, armed with his intuition and the strength of his friends.

Chapter 31

Tomas woke up feeling disoriented. He looked around the unfamiliar room, and his eyes landed on Alex's concerned face.

She asked him how he was feeling, and he replied that he was okay, but he couldn't remember anything after the ritual.

Michael walked in and explained that the ritual was successful, and the darkness was gone, but they needed to figure out how

Tomas had the power to control it. Tomas was shocked; he had no idea he had such a power, let alone how to control

it.

Michael told them that the power was passed down through generations. Tomas' ancestors had acquired the power to manipulate darkness for their benefit but had been consumed by it. Tomas was different; he had the power but had not succumbed to its darkness, making him unique.

Tomas was overwhelmed; he had too many questions and no answers. Michael told him that the answers would come in time, but first, they needed to leave and prepare for the next challenge.

Tomas and his friends left the house, and as they stepped outside, they realized that the world looked different.

Everything was sharper, and the colors were more vibrant. They could feel the presence of the supernatural around them.

Tomas and his friends realized that they had entered a new world, a world that they never knew existed. It was a world full of mysteries and danger, a world that they had to explore.

As they walked away from the house, Tomas had a sense of foreboding; there was still much to be done, and he knew that he had to be ready for it.

The power of intuition had led him here, and he knew that he had to rely on it to face the dangers that lay ahead.

Tomas and his friends walked into the unknown, prepared for whatever lay ahead, ready for the next challenge.

The end was not yet written. Chapter 32

Tomas was in shock. He had always known that there was something different about his family, but he never

E xpected to possess such power. As he and his friends made their way through the unfamiliar world, he couldn't help but feel a sense of

responsibility for what had happened. The darkness had taken hold of him, and he had nearly lost everything.

Michael led them to a small village, where they hoped to find more information. As they walked down the

cobblestone streets, they could feel the eyes of the villagers on them. It was clear that they were outsiders, and they were not welcome.

Tomas suddenly stopped in his tracks, a feeling of dread washing over him. He looked around, trying to find the

source of his unease, but saw nothing out of the ordinary.

"Tomas, what's wrong?" Alex asked, placing a hand on his shoulder.

"I don't know," Tomas replied, his voice barely above a whisper. "Something's not right. We need to be careful." As they continued through the village, they noticed that there were no children playing in the streets, no laughter or music. It was as though the village was cursed, frozen in time.

They eventually reached the town center, where a large gathering had formed. The villagers were huddled

together, murmuring in fear and confusion. Michael

approached them, asking if they knew anything about the darkness that had plagued their world.

One of the villagers stepped forward, a look of fear in his eyes. "It's the curse," he said, his voice barely above a whisper. "The curse of the witch."

Tomas and his friends exchanged worried glances. They knew that they had to find out more about this curse, and fast.

As they delved deeper into the mystery of the cursed village, Tomas felt his intuition sharpening. He was slowly learning to control his power, and it was becoming clearer that his intuition was the key to unlocking the secrets of this world.

But as he delved deeper, he also realized that the darkness was not the only danger lurking in this world. There were other forces at play, and they were just as deadly.

Tomas and his friends knew that they had to be careful, but they also knew that they could not turn their backs on this world. For better or for worse, they were part of it now, and they were the only ones who could stop the darkness from consuming everything.

With that thought in mind, they set out to unravel the mysteries of the cursed village, determined to use their intuition and their newfound power to banish the darkness once and for all.

Chapter 33

As they walked deeper into the cursed village, Tomas couldn't shake the feeling that something was wrong. He didn't know what it was, but his intuition was shouting at him to be careful.

Suddenly, a blood-curdling scream filled the air. They ran towards the sound and found a group of terrified villagers surrounding a young woman who was lying on the ground, her body contorting in unnatural ways.

Tomas felt the darkness stirring within him, urging him to act. He took a deep breath and focused his mind on banishing the evil presence.

As he closed his eyes, he felt a sudden jolt and opened them to find himself standing in the middle of a desolate plain. A figure appeared in the distance, shrouded in shadow.

Tomas knew it was the source of the curse, the very embodiment of evil. He summoned all his courage and charged towards it, his friends close behind.

But as they closed in, the figure shifted and transformed,

revealing itself to be something far more terrifying than they could have ever imagined.

Tomas felt his heart pounding in his chest as the creature towered over them, its eyes glowing with an otherworldly light. But he refused to back down, his intuition and newfound power giving him the strength and determination to face the horror before him.

The creature let out a deafening roar and charged at them, but Tomas stood his ground, his willpower stronger than any fear.

The battle was intense and terrifying, but with the help of his friends, Tomas emerged victorious. The darkness had been banished, the curse lifted.

As they walked away from the cursed village, Tomas knew that there would always be more dangers to face, more darkness to banish. But he was ready, with his intuition and power at his side.

Chapter 34

Eager to leave the cursed village, Tomas and his friends set off down a dusty road, their thoughts consumed with the
horrors they had just witnessed. As they walked, a strange feeling crept up on Tomas - a feeling he had learned to
trust; the power of his intuition. He stopped in his tracks, causing Alex and Lila to halt their conversation and turn to him inquisitively.

"What's wrong, Tomas?" asked Lila, sensing his unease.

"I have a feeling," Tomas replied, his tone grave. "Something feels off about this road."
Alex scoffed, "Tomas, we've been walking on this road for hours. What could be so different now?"
"I don't know," Tomas shrugged, "but I can't shake this feeling. We need to be careful."
As they continued down the road, their surroundings began to shift. The once lush trees and fields transformed into withered and decaying vegetation. The air thickened
with an oppressive aura, and the sky darkened. A sense of dread crept over them, accompanied by an eerie stillness.
Tomas led the way, his senses on high alert, his amulet emitting a faint glow.
Suddenly, a piercing shriek echoed through the air, causing the trio to freeze in fear. A

mangled creature emerged from the darkness, its limbs

twisted and distorted, sharp fangs exposed. Its inhuman eyes fixated on them, a deep growl emanating from deep within its chest.

Despite their fear, Tomas stood his ground, his intuition guiding his actions. He reached within himself, tapping into the power passed down through generations of his

family. His hands began to glow, and with a fierce cry, he unleashed a wave of darkness towards the creature.

The creature shrieked in agony as the wave engulfed it, its form dissipating into nothingness. The oppressive aura

lifted, and the sky brightened once more. Tomas turned to his friends, his expression both amazed and terrified.

"Did you see that?" he asked, his voice shaking.

Alex and Lila stared at him in awe, grateful for their friend's instincts and newfound power.

With a newfound appreciation for the power of intuition, they continued down the road, ready for the dangers that lay ahead.

Chapter 35

As Tomas and his friends walked down the road, the sky turned dark, and the air became cold. Tomas felt a shiver run down his

Spine as he sensed an unsettling presence. He stopped dead

in his tracks and turned around. Something was following

them, creeping in the shadows. He couldn't see what it was, but he knew it was there, watching them.

"Tomas, what's wrong?" Lila asked, noticing the worried expression on his face.

"We're not alone," Tomas replied, his voice barely above a whisper.

Alex and Lila exchanged a nervous glance as they looked around, trying to spot what was bothering Tomas.

Suddenly, a blood-curdling scream filled the air, making them jump. It was coming from behind them, and it was getting closer. They turned around, and they saw a terrifying sight.

A group of dark spirits had appeared out of nowhere, hovering in front of them, their faces twisted into grotesque expressions. They were hissing and growling, their eyes glowing with malevolence. Tomas raised his amulet, but he knew it wouldn't be enough to defeat them all.

"We have to run!" Tomas shouted, grabbing his friends' hands and pulling them along with him. They started running, but the spirits were following them, their spectral forms gliding through the air.

As they ran, Tomas's intuition kicked in, and he knew what he had to do. He slowed down, making his friends stop too.

"What are you doing?" Alex asked, panting.

"Tomas, we can't stop!" Lila added, her voice shaking.

"Trust me," Tomas said, his eyes closed in concentration. He raised his hand and whispered something under his breath.

Suddenly, the spirits stopped in midair, as if frozen. They were confused and disoriented, unable to move or attack.

Tomas opened his eyes and smiled at his friends. "Let's go," he said, and they started running again, leaving the spirits behind.

As they ran, Tomas couldn't help but wonder what other horrors awaited them on their journey. But he was determined to face them, using his intuition and his newfound power to banish the darkness and protect his friends.

Chapter 36

As they continued their journey, Tomas found it increasingly difficult to ignore the nagging feeling that something was off. Despite the calming presence of his
friends, he felt a cold sensation creeping up his spine. He decided to voice his concerns to Alex and Lila.

"I don't know guys," he said, "Something feels wrong. We should be on high alert."

Alex and Lila glanced at each other with concern etched on their faces. They knew better than to ignore Tomas's intuition, especially after all they had been through.

They continued walking down the path in silence, their senses heightened and their eyes darting around for any sign of danger. Suddenly, the dense forest around them
began to thin out, and they found themselves standing at the edge of a vast, open field.

But the moment they stepped into the field, they felt it. The air grew thick and heavy, and a sense of impending doom descended upon them. They all froze in their tracks, their eyes focused on the horizon.

And then they saw it. A dark figure, looming in the distance. It was moving steadily towards them, and as it drew closer, they could
make out its grotesque features.

It was a creature unlike any they had ever seen before. Its skin was a sickly gray, and its eyes glowed a fiery red. It was hunched over, and its long, spindly fingers dragged along the ground as it
walked.

Tomas felt a sudden rush of fear, but he knew he had to stay focused. He closed his eyes, and took a deep breath.

When he opened them again, he had a newfound sense of clarity.

He raised his hand and pointed it at the creature, and with a surge of energy, he unleashed a beam of light. The creature screeched in agony as it was consumed by the light, and when it dissipated, it was gone.

Alex and Lila looked at Tomas in awe, amazed by the power he possessed. But Tomas knew that this was just the beginning. He had a feeling that more challenges lay ahead, and he was ready to face them head-on.

Chapter 37

Tomas, Alex, and Lila had been on the road for hours, with no sign of civilization or any other living being. The only sound was the rustling of leaves and the crunching of

sticks under their feet. Tomas had a sinking feeling in his

gut, but he tried to shake it off. He had been wrong before about his intuition, maybe he was just being paranoid.

But then, a deafening roar shattered the silence. The three friends stopped in their tracks, their eyes wide with fear.

The sound echoed through the woods and sent chills down their spines. Tomas knew right away that it was not a natural sound. It was something otherworldly, something sinister.

As they stood frozen, a dark figure appeared in the distance. It was massive, with long, sharp claws and

glowing red eyes. It was like nothing they had ever seen before. The figure let out another deafening roar, and a

gust of wind knocked Tomas and his friends off their feet.

Tomas scrambled to his feet, his heart racing. He knew that they had to run. They had to get away from this monster, or they would

not make it out alive. Tomas led the charge, sprinting as

fast as he could through the woods. Alex and Lila followed close behind, their breaths coming in short gasps.

The creature pursued them, crashing through the trees and leaving destruction in its wake. Tomas could hear its roars getting closer and closer, and he knew they were running out of time.

Just when they thought they were done for, they saw a glimmer of light in the distance. It was their only hope. They sprinted towards it, with the creature hot on their heels.

As they approached the light, they saw that it was coming from a small cabin. Tomas banged on the door, screaming for help. The door swung open, and an old woman appeared, her face etched with worry.

"Come in, quickly!" she shouted.

The three friends stumbled into the cabin, panting and sweating. The woman slammed the door shut, and Tomas could feel the creature's presence looming just outside.

"What was that thing?" Lila gasped.

"It was a demon," the woman said, her voice heavy with dread. "The most powerful one I've ever encountered."

Tomas knew that they were not safe. Not yet. The demon was still out there, waiting for them. But he also knew that

his intuition had not failed him. He had felt that something was wrong, and he had been right. Now, they had to figure out a way to defeat the demon, or else it would be the end of them all.

Chapter 38

Tomas, Alex, and Lila huddled together, their hearts racing as they listened to the old woman's words. "You must find the demon's true name," she said, her voice barely above a whisper. "Once you have it, you can command it to leave."

"But how do we find its name?" Alex asked, her voice trembling.

The old woman leaned forward, her eyes locking onto Tomas's. "You already know it," she said. "It's inside you."

Tomas felt a chill run down his spine. "What do you mean?"

"The demon knows your darkest fear," the old woman continued. "It whispers it to you every night, and you try to ignore it. But now you must confront it. Face your fear, and the demon's name will be revealed."

Tomas swallowed hard, knowing exactly what the old woman was talking about. He had always been plagued by nightmares of drowning, a fear that had paralyzed him since childhood.

Without a word, he turned and walked out of the cabin, towards the nearby lake. Alex and Lila followed, their eyes wide with fear.

Tomas stood on the shore, staring out at the dark water. He closed his eyes and took a deep breath, trying to steady his nerves. Then, with a sudden burst of courage, he stepped into the water.

It was freezing, and the shock of it almost took his breath away. But he kept walking, the water rising higher and higher until it reached his chest.

He could feel the fear creeping in, the memories of his nightmares flooding his mind. But he pushed them aside, focusing on the demon's name.

And then, suddenly, it came to him. A word he had never heard before, but one that felt like it had been inside him all along.

He opened his eyes and looked back at Alex and Lila, who were watching him anxiously from the shore. "I have it," he said, his voice steady. "The demon's name."

They returned to the cabin, where the old woman gave them instructions on how to perform the ritual to banish the demon. Tomas spoke the demon's true name with conviction, and they chanted together, their amulets glowing brightly.

Slowly, the cabin began to shake, and the air grew thick with darkness. But they held fast, their wills unbreakable. And finally, with a deafening roar, the demon was gone.

They collapsed in a heap on the floor, panting and exhausted. But they were alive, and they had defeated the demon.

Tomas looked at his friends, a sense of pride swelling inside him. He had always trusted his intuition, but now he knew that it was more than just a feeling. It was a source of power, a force that could overcome even the darkest of evils.

And he was ready to face whatever came next.

Chapter 39

Tomas, Alex, and Lila had finally banished the demon and felt relieved. However, they were left with the nagging

feeling that there was still something they had missed. As

They made their way out of the cabin, they noticed that the sky had darkened, and a fierce wind had picked up. Tomas checked his amulet and realized that the conjured protection circle had been broken; they were no longer safe.

The old woman warned them of a dark forest nearby, where evil spirits and demons were said to reside. She

urged them to leave the area immediately, but the group

knew they had to face the danger head-on. They couldn't let the evil fester and grow stronger.

As they ventured deeper into the woods, they could feel the malevolent presence growing stronger. Strange noises and whispers echoed around them, and the trees seemed to take on a sinister, twisted appearance. The group remained quiet as they walked, weapons at the ready. They knew that they couldn't let their guard down for even a second.

It wasn't long before they came upon a clearing where a group of twisted, dark creatures were waiting for them. They seemed to be feeding on a dead animal, and their eyes glowed with a sickly green light. The creatures screeched as they attacked, and the group fought back with all their might. Tomas used his intuition and his newfound power

to conjure beams of light that scattered the creatures. Alex and Lila fought alongside him, watching each other's backs.

However, it wasn't enough. The creatures had called forth a powerful demon that emerged from the darkness,

towering over them like a giant. The demon's eyes gleamed with a fierce red light, and his skin shimmered like black ice. Tomas realized that this was the true source of the malevolent presence they had been sensing all along.

The group stood no chance against such a powerful entity, but they knew they had to try. They fought with all their might, but the demon laughed at their efforts. Tomas

realized that he had to call upon his intuition once again,

tapping into a deeper power within himself. He focused on the demon's true name, and a piercing beam of light shot out of his hand, striking the demon's chest. The demon roared in pain as he was banished back to the darkness he had come from.

Panting and battered, the group made their way out of the forest, exhausted but triumphant. They knew that they had faced tremendous evil and prevailed, but they also knew

that there was still work to be done. They had to remain vigilant, always on the lookout

for signs of darkness lurking in the shadows. The power of intuition had saved them once again, but they couldn't rest on their laurels. The battle against evil was a never-ending one, and they were ready to face whatever was to come.

Chapter 40

Tomas, Alex, and Lila sat around a small fire, discussing their recent victory and how they had managed to banish the demon. The group was exhausted, both mentally and physically, after the ordeal in the forest.

Suddenly, Tomas sat upright, his eyes widening as he felt a chill run down his spine. He knew that feeling all too well – it was his intuition warning him of danger.

"We're not alone," he said, his voice barely above a whisper. His companions looked at him in confusion, but before they could ask any questions, a deafening roar echoed through the forest.

The group scrambled to their feet, preparing themselves for battle. They could hear footsteps approaching and the sound of rasping breaths.

Tomas's intuition kicked into overdrive, and he knew that they needed to act fast if they wanted to survive. He quickly conjured a protection circle around them, chanting in a language none of them understood.

Alex and Lila watched in amazement as the circle lit up, forming a barrier of light around them. They could see dark figures lurking at the edge of the circle, trying to break through.

Suddenly, something hit the barrier with incredible force, causing it to flicker and fade. The trio knew they had to act quickly if they wanted to maintain their protection.

Tomas reached deep within himself, tapping into his intuition and calling upon the power of the artifacts they had collected on their journey. He chanted words of power, his voice growing louder and more frantic.

As he spoke, the circle began to pulse with energy, and the dark figures outside recoiled, hissing and snarling in fury.

The trio watched in amazement as the figures began to dissolve, their forms breaking apart like smoke in the wind. The roar that had filled the forest quieted, replaced by a deafening silence.

The protection circle flickered and faded, leaving Tomas,

Alex, and Lila standing alone in the clearing. They knew that they had narrowly escaped death, and that their journey was far from over.

Tomas looked at his companions, his eyes filled with determination. "We can do this," he said. "We have the power of intuition on our side, and we will defeat whatever comes our way."

Alex and Lila nodded, their expressions set in determination. They knew that their journey was far from over, but they were more determined than ever to face whatever lay ahead.

Chapter 41

The trio had been on the road for weeks, traveling from one town to another, searching for supernatural entities that needed to be banished. The constant fighting against dark forces had taken a toll on their minds and bodies, leaving them exhausted and on edge.
One day, they stumbled upon a small town that seemed to be frozen in time. The streets were lined with charming

Cottages, and the locals were warm and welcoming. Tomas, Alex, and Lila decided to take a break from their mission and enjoy the tranquility of the town.
They spent their days exploring the town's hidden nooks and crannies, trying out local delicacies, and getting to know the friendly locals. For the first time in weeks, they felt like they could breathe again.

One evening, they were invited to a bonfire hosted by the townspeople. As they sat around the fire, listening to the locals' stories and songs, Tomas realized that they had

been so focused on their mission that they had forgotten how to enjoy life's simple pleasures.
He turned to his friends and said, "You know, we've been so caught up in fighting evil that we forgot what we're fighting for."
Alex and Lila nodded in agreement, and they sat around the fire, basking in the warmth and joy of the moment. For the first time in weeks, they felt like they had finally found a sense of peace.
As they walked back to their lodgings, they laughed and joked, feeling like their burdens had been lifted. They had

forgotten what it felt like to be carefree, but now they knew that they could still find happiness in life's simplest moments.

The town had given them a much-needed break, and they were grateful for it. But their journey was far from over, and they knew that they would soon have to face more evil and darkness.

However, for now, they were content to enjoy the lightness and joy that the town had given them. They slept soundly that night, feeling like they had finally found a sense of peace in their tumultuous journey.

Chapter 42

Tomas woke up in a cold sweat, his heart racing. He couldn't shake off the feeling that something was off. He
looked around the room, but there was nothing out of the ordinary. Alex and Lila were still asleep in their beds, and the sun was peeking through the curtains. He took a deep breath and tried to calm himself down but couldn't shake off the feeling that they were being watched.
He got up and walked to the window, peering outside. The town was quiet and peaceful. It was exactly what they needed after the last few weeks of chaos and danger. He rubbed his tired eyes and
decided to take a stroll around town to clear his head.

As he walked, he noticed that the town seemed deserted.

There were no people on the streets, no kids playing in the parks, and all the stores were closed. It was as if everyone
had vanished. He checked his watch and realized that it was only 9 am. It didn't make any sense.
Suddenly, he heard a faint whispering coming from an alleyway. He followed the sound, and as he turned the
C orner, he saw a group of hooded figures standing in front
of a large, ominous building. The figures were chanting in a language he couldn't understand, and he could feel their dark energy radiating from them. He cautiously approached them, but they didn't seem to notice him. He recognized the building as an old
abandoned church that he had read about in the town's history. The building seemed to be emitting a strange and powerful energy.

Tomas knew he had to act fast. He quickly retrieved the map that Adam had given him and studied it closely. He saw that there was another artifact nearby, one that he had not yet found. The map led him to a nearby cemetery where he discovered the artifact, an old tombstone with obscure symbols engraved on it.

As he picked it up, he felt a surge of energy, and his intuition kicked in. He knew what he had to do. He raced back to the church and entered it with confidence. The hooded figures turned around, and their red eyes stared at him with fury.

With the power of the artifact and his intuition, Tomas was able to banish the dark spirits from the church and seal the building with a powerful protection spell. As the energy dissipated, he heard a faint voice whisper, "You have only delayed the inevitable."

Tomas knew that this battle was far from over. He left the church, feeling proud of his intuition and the power of the artifacts, but also aware that there were more challenges ahead. The trio had to stick together and prepare for whatever was coming next.

Chapter 43

Tomas sighed in relief as the last of the dark spirits dissipated into the night. He knew that this was only a temporary victory and that more challenges lay ahead. As he turned to leave, he heard a sound behind him. It was a

S oft rustling, as if someone was walking through the fallen leaves. He glanced around but saw nothing. He dismissed it and walked back to the inn where Alex and Lila were staying.

The next morning, they decided to leave the town and continue their journey. As they packed their belongings, Tomas felt a strange sensation in his pocket. It was the artifact he had used to banish the spirits last night. He had forgotten to return it to its resting place. He pulled it out of his pocket and examined it closely. Its surface was smooth and cold, and he could feel a faint pulse of energy emanating from it.

Just as he was about to put it back in his pocket, the artifact began to glow. The light grew brighter and brighter until it was almost blinding. Suddenly, the artifact exploded, sending shards of metal flying in all directions. Tomas, Alex, and Lila leaped to their feet and ducked for cover.

When the ringing in their ears subsided, they cautiously emerged from their hiding places. What they saw made their blood run cold. The inn was surrounded by a horde of dark spirits, their eyes aglow with malice. The trio knew they were outnumbered and out-matched.

In the midst of the chaos, Tomas felt a strange sensation in the pit of his stomach. It was a feeling he knew all too well - the power of
intuition. He closed his eyes and focused, tuning out the chaos around him. Suddenly, he knew what to do.
He reached into his pocket and pulled out the remaining artifacts.
He spread them out on the ground and began to chant an ancient incantation. At first, nothing happened. Then, one by one, the artifacts began to glow with a faint blue light. The light grew brighter and brighter until it was almost blinding.
Suddenly, a wave of energy swept through the inn, knocking the dark spirits off their feet. The trio watched in awe as the spirits writhed in pain, their flesh scorched by the power of the artifacts. When it was over, the spirits were gone, and the inn was once again peaceful.
Tomas, Alex, and Lila looked at each other in disbelief.
They had never seen anything like it. The power of intuition and the ancient artifacts had saved them once
again. But they knew that their journey was far from over, and that the forces of darkness were always lurking just around the corner.

Chapter 44

Tomas, Alex, and Lila continued their journey through the wilderness, following the map that would lead them to the next artifact. They had faced many obstacles and dangers
over the past few weeks, but they were still determined to put an end to the malevolent force that threatened their world.

As they walked, Tomas couldn't shake the feeling that they were being watched. He had always trusted his intuition, and it had saved them from countless dangers so far. He

stopped and looked around, but there was nothing there.

Still, he couldn't shake the feeling of unease.
Suddenly, a dark cloud appeared above them, and the wind picked up, howling through the trees. Tomas knew that
this was no coincidence. He reached for one of his artifacts and held it tightly in his hand, ready for whatever was to come.
And then, they saw it. A massive, shadowy figure towering over them, its eyes glowing red in the darkness. The trio froze in terror as the figure approached them, its footsteps shaking the ground
beneath their feet.
Tomas took a step forward, holding up the artifact and calling upon its power. The figure roared in anger and
lunged at him, but Tomas was ready. He dodged the attack and struck the figure with the artifact, sending it reeling backwards.

Alex and Lila joined in the fight, wielding ancient weapons and spells to weaken the figure. It was a fierce battle, each of them using their skills to gain the upper hand. But

finally, they emerged victorious, the figure defeated and banished from their world.

As they caught their breath, Tomas realized that their journey was far from over. There were more artifacts to find, more battles to fight. But he knew that they would

face them all together, relying on their intuition and skills to defeat even the most overwhelming of foes.

And so, the trio set out once again, determined to put an end to the malevolent force that threatened their world, no matter what it took.

Chapter 45

Tomas, Alex, and Lila trudged through the dense forest, their breaths coming out in gasps as they tried to keep up with Tomas's brisk pace. They had been walking for what

felt like hours, with no sign of civilization in sight. The canopy of trees above them blocked out most of the

sunlight, casting eerie shadows on the forest floor.

Tomas had a feeling that they were being followed, but he couldn't be sure. He couldn't shake the feeling of unease that had settled in his gut since they had left the small

town. He had seen too much on their journey, and he knew that they were never truly safe.

Suddenly, they heard a rustling in the bushes behind them. Tomas whirled around, his hand instinctively reaching for the ancient

dagger strapped to his thigh. Alex and Lila followed suit, their hands hovering over their own weapons.

But instead of an attacker, they found a small, dirty-faced boy staring up at them with wide eyes. He couldn't have been more than six or seven years old, and his ragged

clothing and hollow cheeks spoke of a lifetime of poverty.

"What are you doing out here, all alone?" Lila asked gently, crouching down to the boy's level.

The boy hesitated for a moment before speaking, his voice barely above a whisper. "I'm lost. I was following the butterflies, and then I got lost." He pointed to a group of colorful insects fluttering above him.

Tomas looked around warily. Something about the situation didn't sit right with him. "We need to keep moving. It's not safe here."

But Lila was already taking charge. "We can't just leave him here. We'll take him with us, at least until we can find his family."

Tomas reluctantly agreed, and they added the boy to their group. They walked for hours, and Tomas's intuition kept him on high alert. They encountered no other dangers, but the feeling of unease remained.

As the sun began to set, they came across an old, abandoned cabin. It looked rundown and abandoned, but it was the best shelter they had found so far. They settled in for the night, with the boy curled up in a makeshift bed made of blankets and pine needles.

But as they drifted off to sleep, Tomas felt a presence in the cabin. He knew they weren't alone.

Chapter 46

Tomas couldn't shake the feeling of being watched as they settled into the abandoned cabin. The lost boy, who they discovered was named Timmy, seemed unfazed by the eerie atmosphere. But as the sun set, the feeling of being watched intensified.

Tomas decided to explore the cabin, hoping to find some clue as to what was causing his unease. He found nothing out of the ordinary. Just an old, rundown cabin with creaky floorboards and dusty furniture. But as he turned to leave the room, he noticed something odd about the wall.

There was a small crack in the wood paneling, barely noticeable. Tomas' intuition told him to investigate further. He pushed at the crack, and the paneling gave way with a creak.

Behind the paneling was a hidden room. In the center of the room was a small altar, adorned with candles and

Strange symbols. Tomas felt a wave of fear wash over him. The presence he had felt earlier was coming from this very room.

As he stepped towards the altar, he heard a voice in his mind. It was a raspy, otherworldly voice, urging him to perform a ritual. Tomas knew that this was dangerous, that he should leave and forget he ever found this room. But his intuition told him that this was the key to stopping the darkness.

He reached for the ornate box they had acquired, knowing that this was the moment they had been searching for. He opened the box and felt the dark energy flowing through his veins.

Tomas began to chant, matching the strange symbols on the altar. The candle flames flickered as the air around him grew thick with an ominous energy. Suddenly, the room shook, and the candles went out.

The darkness was gone.

Tomas felt a wave of relief wash over him as he left the hidden room. His intuition had once again led him to victory, but he knew that there were still more challenges ahead.

As they settled in for the night, Tomas couldn't help but wonder what was waiting for them in the morning. But for now, he was content in the knowledge that they were one step closer to ending the darkness that had haunted them for so long.

Chapter 47

The next morning, Tomas woke up with a feeling of unease. He couldn't shake the feeling that something was watching them. He looked around the room and noticed that the boy they had found was nowhere to be seen. He shook Alex awake and told her to look for the boy while he investigated the rest of the cabin.

As he walked through the cabin, he heard strange noises coming from the hidden room he had discovered the night before. He cautiously approached the room and saw the

ornate box he had used in the ritual was open, and the boy was standing in front of it. Tomas could sense the dark energy emanating from the box and knew that the boy had been drawn to it.

"Tomas, what's going on?" Alex asked, appearing behind him.

"The boy, he's drawn to the box," Tomas replied, pointing to the open box.

Just then, the room began to shake, and the symbols on the altar glowed red. A dark mist started to pour out of the box, engulfing the boy. Tomas and Alex rushed to his side, but it was too late. The boy had been possessed by the dark energy.

The possessed boy lunged at Tomas, who managed to dodge him and grab his bag. He pulled out an ancient book of spells and began reciting an incantation to banish the dark energy. Alex stood at his side, holding a sword ready to strike if needed.

The possessed boy let out an ear-piercing scream as the dark energy was banished from his body. He collapsed to the ground and lay there unconscious.

"We need to take him with us," Tomas said, picking up the boy.

"But what about the box?" Alex asked, looking at the ornate box.

"We'll have to take it with us too," Tomas replied, placing the box in his bag. As they left the cabin, Tomas couldn't shake the feeling that they were being watched. He knew that their journey was far from over, and they still had a long way to go before they could finally defeat the darkness once and for all.

Chapter 48

As they continued their journey, the group felt a sense of unease, each lost in their own thoughts. Tomas couldn't shake off the feeling that something was off, that they were being watched.

The forest around them seemed to grow denser, making it difficult for them to advance. A thick mist surrounded them, obscuring their vision and making it hard for them to navigate. As they walked, they heard strange noises, like voices whispering in the fog.

Tomas knew they were getting close to the next artifact, and the darkness seemed to be closing in on them. He felt a tug on the ornate box he was carrying, and he knew that the darkness was trying to get its hands on it.

Suddenly, Lila cried out, and they all turned to see her being pulled into the mist. Tomas saw the look of terror on her face as she disappeared from view. Without hesitation, Tomas sprinted towards where Lila had been, calling out her name. Alex followed behind him, ready for whatever lay ahead.

As they ran, the whispers grew louder, and Tomas could feel the malevolent force surrounding them. He knew that they were in grave danger, and that their lives were at stake.

Finally, they reached a clearing, where Lila was being held captive by a group of shadowy figures. Tomas recognized them from his earlier encounter, and he knew that they were under the control of the darkness.

Without a second thought, he raised the ornate box and began to chant the spell that he had used earlier. He felt the power rush through him, and he watched as the darkness was expelled from the figures.

They collapsed to the ground, and Tomas felt a sense of relief wash over him. He had saved his friends once again, but he knew that the darkness was still out there, waiting for them.

As they continued on their journey, they knew that they would face even more challenges along the way. But they had hope, and they had each other, and they knew that if they stayed true to their instincts, they would overcome whatever lay ahead.

Chapter 49

Tomas, Alex, and Lila continued their journey through the forest, feeling the weight of their mission on their
shoulders. Their nerves were on edge, but they were

determined to see it through to the end. As they walked,

they noticed that the trees around them began to thin out, revealing a bright blue sky above.
The group walked out of the dense forest and into an open meadow. The sun was shining down on them, and they
couldn't help but feel lighter with each step. Birds chirped in the nearby trees, and a gentle breeze rustled the tall grass around them.
Tomas felt a weight lifted from his shoulders, and he knew that the darkness was no longer surrounding them. He
looked at Alex and Lila, who were both wearing broad smiles on their faces.
They
all knew that the worst was behind them, and they were filled with hope for what came next.

As they walked, they saw a small village in the distance.

Tomas had a feeling that they would find what they were looking for there.
The group picked up their pace, eager to find some answers.
As they entered the village, they saw friendly faces and warm, welcoming homes. Children ran through the streets,

laughing and playing, and the group couldn't help but feel overjoyed. They knew that, with the help of the village, they could finally put an end to the darkness that had been haunting them.

Tomas knew that his intuition had brought them this far and that it would guide them to the end. He looked at his

companions, who now felt like family, and knew that they

were in this together. They would stop at nothing to rid the world of the darkness that had threatened to destroy them.

The group continued their journey, feeling lighter and more hopeful than ever before. They knew that they would

face challenges ahead, but they were ready for whatever lay ahead. They had the power of intuition on their side, and they knew that it would lead them to victory.

Chapter 50

As Tomas, Alex, and Lila walked through the friendly village, they felt a sense of relief wash over them. The

people they encountered were warm and welcoming, and

they were invited to stay in a cozy inn for the night. For the first time in what felt like ages, they were able to relax and enjoy each other's company. Over dinner, they discussed their next steps. They knew they needed to find another artifact, but they also realized they needed to take a moment to catch their breath. Tomas recommended they spend a few days in the village, getting to know the

locals and taking advantage of the peaceful surroundings.

As they explored the village, they discovered that it was known for its healing springs. Curious, they decided to visit the springs and were amazed by what they found. The

water was crystal clear and felt rejuvenating on their skin.

They spent hours lounging by the water and soaking in the healing properties of the springs. That night, they returned to the inn feeling refreshed and renewed. As they got ready for bed, Tomas couldn't help but notice how much lighter the atmosphere felt. The sense of impending doom that had been following them for so long seemed to have dissipated, at least for the time being.

As he drifted off to sleep, Tomas felt a sense of gratitude for his intuition and the bond he had formed with Alex and Lila. Despite the challenges they had faced and those that undoubtedly lay ahead, he felt confident that they would prevail as long as they trusted in themselves and their instincts.

Chapter 51

Tomas, Alex, and Lila spent their days in the village getting to know the locals and enjoying the simple pleasures of
life. They ate delicious meals, swam in the healing springs, and listened to the stories of the villagers. They felt relieved to be in a place of safety after the terrors of the forest.

During their stay, they heard about an old hermit who lived on the outskirts of the village. He was said to be wise
beyond his years and had a reputation for helping those in need. Curiosity got the better of Tomas, and he decided to seek out the hermit's advice.

The hermit's dwelling was a small hut on the edge of the forest. It was dark inside and smelled of herbs and incense.

The hermit sat on the floor, surrounded by scrolls and candles. He looked up at Tomas, his eyes twinkling with hidden knowledge.

"What brings you to my humble abode?" he asked.

Tomas explained their situation, about the malevolent force they were facing and their mission to find the artifacts.

The hermit listened intently before nodding his head. "You are on a noble quest, but be warned. The path ahead is
treacherous, and not all will make it out alive. However, I have faith in your intuition. Follow your instincts, and you will prevail."

With these parting words, the hermit sent Tomas on his way feeling a renewed sense of purpose. He returned to the village, where Alex and Lila were waiting eagerly for news.

Together, they made plans for the next leg of their journey, ready to face whatever lay ahead with the power of intuition on their side.

Chapter 52

Tomas woke up in the middle of the night to the sound of rustling outside their cottage. His intuition immediately
kicked in, and he sat up, listening closely. He heard a faint whimper, and his heart raced as he got up to investigate.
Lila and Alex were sound asleep, so he quietly slipped out of the door and into the darkness.
He followed the sound to the forest's edge, where he found a young boy, no older than six, huddled in fear against a
tree. The boy was shivering, and his clothes were torn and covered in dirt. Tomas knelt down and asked the boy what had happened.
The boy's face was ashen as he spoke of a dark figure that had dragged him out of his bed and into the forest. Tomas felt a chill run down his spine as he realized that the darkness was still after them.
He picked the boy up and brought him back to the cottage, where Alex and Lila were now awake. The boy was given food and water, and they listened as he spoke of the shadows attacking the village.
Tomas knew that they had to act fast before the darkness grew stronger.
The group packed their bags and set out into the forest, following
the trails of destruction left by the shadows. As they

walked, they felt the darkness closing in, threatening to

suffocate them. But Tomas's intuition kept them focused, and they soon found themselves standing before a massive tree.

The tree was gnarled, with twisted branches that seemed to reach out like claws. It was surrounded by a thick fog that obscured everything beyond a few feet. Tomas knew that this was the source of the darkness, and that they had to face it head-on if they were to save the village.

He reached out and grabbed Lila and Alex's hands, feeling their strength and determination. Together, they stepped into the fog, ready to face whatever lay ahead.

Chapter 53

As the trio moved deeper into the forest, they heard a woman's voice calling for help. Tomas took the lead, his intuition guiding him through the thick trees and
overgrown bushes. Finally, they came upon a clearing where they saw a young woman tied to a tree with a gag in her mouth.

Without hesitation, they rushed to her aid, untying her and removing the gag. The woman, named Emily, was shaken and disoriented. She explained that she had been hiking alone when she was attacked and taken captive by a group of dark-cloaked figures.

Tomas, Alex, and Lila listened intently as Emily described her captors and the location of their lair. They knew that they had to act fast to stop the dark energy from spreading any further.

Together, the group set off towards the lair, their determination fueling their steps. As they approached, they could feel the oppressive energy emanating from the decrepit building.

Tomas led the charge, his intuition guiding him towards the heart of the darkness. As they entered the lair, they were immediately
confronted by the dark-cloaked figures that had attacked them before. But this time, they were ready.

With the power of their intuition and the strength of their bond, Tomas, Alex, Lila, and Emily fought back against the malevolent force. The battle was fierce, but they emerged victorious, the darkness vanishing in a burst of light.

As they stood there, catching their breath and surveying the damage, they knew that their journey was far from over. But with each other and the power of their intuition by their side, they felt ready to face whatever challenges lay ahead.

Chapter 54

Tomas wakes up in a cold sweat, his intuition telling him something is wrong. He looks around the cozy cottage, but everything appears normal. Alex and Lila are still sleeping soundly beside him, and the rescued boy is snuggled up in blankets on the floor. Tomas tries to shake off the feeling and closes his eyes, hoping to fall back asleep.

But then he hears it, a faint whisper coming from the corner of the room. Tomas opens his eyes to see a shadowy figure standing by the window, its back to him. The figure turns slowly, revealing a twisted, demonic face that chills Tomas to the bone.

Tomas jumps out of bed, waking up Alex and Lila. They stare in horror as the figure materializes into a full-bodied demon, its skin charred and glowing with an unholy light.

The demon speaks in a voice that sounds like a thousand tortured souls. "You have trespassed in my realm. You must pay the price."

Tomas, Alex, and Lila huddle together, trying to stay strong in the face of such malevolence. Tomas' intuition tells him that they must fight with all their might, or else
they will be lost to the
demon's grasp forever.

The trio stands their ground, using all of their intuition and strength to fight back against the demon's onslaught.

They chant ancient words of power, calling forth their own inner strength and the strength of the universe.

The demon fights back with equal ferocity, but the bond between the three friends is unbreakable. Together, they manage to weaken the demon and banish it back to its own realm.

Tomas collapses onto the floor, exhausted but relieved that they were able to defeat such a powerful foe. He knows that they can never let their guard down, that they must always be aware of the darkness that lurks in the world.

As they gather their strength and prepare to continue their journey, Tomas takes comfort in the fact that they have each other and their intuition to guide them. No matter what horrors lie ahead, they will face them together.

Chapter 55

Tomas knew it was a mistake to let their guard down, even for a moment. They had defeated the dark-cloaked figures and banished the demon, but he could feel that the darkness was still lingering, waiting for the right opportunity to strike again.

As he lay in bed, trying to shake off the uneasy feeling, he heard a soft whisper in his ear. He sat up, heart racing, but the room was empty. He convinced himself it was just his imagination and lay down again.

But then he felt a cold breath on his neck, and he turned to see a figure standing at the foot of his bed. It was a woman, but her features were twisted and grotesque, like a monstrous mockery of humanity. Tomas tried to scream, but no sound came out of his mouth. The figure leaned in closer, and he could feel its icy breath on his face.

Then, just as suddenly as it had appeared, the figure disappeared. Tomas lay there, shaking and sweating, trying to convince himself it was just a nightmare. But deep down, he knew that it was real, and that the darkness was still out there, waiting for them.

He got out of bed, determined to keep his friends safe. They needed to be ready for whatever came next, and they

Needed to rely on their intuition and their bond to survive.

The next morning, as they sat around the breakfast table,

Tomas told his companions what had happened. Alex and Lila listened in silence, their faces pale and serious.

"We can't let our guard down again," Alex said. "We need to be prepared for whatever comes next."

Lila nodded. "We need to stay together and trust each other, no matter what."

Tomas felt a sense of reassurance knowing that he wasn't alone in this fight. They would face the darkness together, with their intuition and their bond as their weapons.

But he also knew that the terror he had experienced in the night was just the beginning. There was something out there, something powerful and malevolent, that was coming for them. And they needed to be ready.

Chapter 56

Tomas couldn't shake the feeling that something was off. He had barely slept all night, his mind consumed with thoughts of the twisted woman and the whisper in his ear. His intuition was telling him that danger was near, but he couldn't pinpoint where it was coming from.

As he stepped out of the cottage and into the misty morning, he felt the weight of the previous night's events bearing down on him. He couldn't let his guard down. Not now.

As he walked deeper into the woods, he heard the snap of a twig. He turned around, but saw nothing. His heart began to race as he realized he was being watched.

Tomas' intuition kicked into high gear. He knew that whoever was following him was not friendly. He started to jog back towards the cottage, but the rustling in the brush grew louder and closer.

Suddenly, a figure stepped out from behind a tree. It was the twisted woman from his nightmare.

"You shouldn't have destroyed my lair," she hissed. "You'll pay for what you've done."

Tomas knew he had to act quickly. He focused all of his energy on his intuition, feeling the power surge through him. He could see the darkness within the woman, and knew that he had to banish it.

With a fierce determination, Tomas channeled his intuition and pushed the darkness out of the woman. She screamed and thrashed, but eventually collapsed onto the forest floor, her body writhing in pain.

Tomas breathed a sigh of relief, knowing that he had saved himself and his companions once again. But he also knew that there was still more darkness out there, waiting to strike.

As he walked back to the cottage, Tomas made a silent vow to always trust his intuition, no matter how dangerous the situation. He knew that the power of intuition was the only thing that could

keep him and his friends safe from the horrors that lurked in the darkness.

Chapter 57

Tomas's intuition proved to be correct as danger lurked around every corner. He and his friends were on edge

B ecause they could sense something sinister approaching. They had been traveling for hours, searching for the final artifact that could put an end to the darkness that threatened their existence.

As they walked, the wind picked up, and the air turned icy cold. The sky darkened, and the once-green trees now

looked dead. Tomas, Alex, and Lila could feel their hearts racing as fear crept up their spines.

"Just keep moving forward," Tomas urged, his voice shaking slightly. "We can't let it get us."

They continued through the woods, trying to ignore the strange noises and rustling of leaves around them. As they walked, they came across a clearing, and in the middle of it stood a twisted old tree.

Tomas's intuition kicked in, and he knew that this was the place they had been searching for. His heart pounding, he approached the tree, and his friends followed.

But as they got closer, the ground shook, and they heard a deafening roar. Suddenly, a massive creature appeared,

towering above them. Its skin was as black as coal, and its eyes glowed red with malice.

The friends stood frozen, but Tomas knew what he had to do. He remembered the lessons he had learned throughout his journey and trusted his intuition. Steeling his nerves, he held the magical artifact and chanted the ancient words that he had memorized.

As he spoke, the creature grew weaker, and the darkness around them dissipated. Finally, it let out a final roar and disappeared from sight.

Tomas and his friends stood there, breathing heavily, knowing that they had triumphed over the darkness. They were a team, and together they had defeated what seemed like an unstoppable force.

As they left the clearing, Tomas knew that although the darkness may still exist, he had the power to combat it.

With his intuition as his guide, he knew that he would always be prepared to face whatever lay ahead.

Chapter 58

As Tomas and his friends walked through the woods, they couldn't shake the feeling that they were being watched.

Tomas's intuition was on high alert, and he silently signaled to Alex and Lila to stay sharp and stay together.

As they reached a clearing, they spotted movement in the trees. Tomas squinted, trying to see through the darkness, and suddenly felt a jolt of fear run through him.

"Guys, we need to move," he said urgently. "Something's coming."

They picked up their pace, but whatever was following them seemed to be gaining ground. Tomas heard the sound of twigs snapping and leaves rustling behind them, and he knew they were running out of time.

"Stop!" he shouted. "We can't outrun it. We have to face it."

Alex and Lila looked at him, fear etched on their faces. But they knew better than to argue with Tomas's intuition.

They turned to face whatever was behind them, ready to fight.

Out of the darkness stepped a figure. It was a woman, dressed in tattered clothes and covered in dirt and grime.

Her eyes were sunken and dark, and her hair hung in matted clumps around her face.

Tomas's intuition told him that this woman was more than just a lost traveler. She was a danger, a manifestation of the darkness they had been fighting against.

"Who are you?" Tomas demanded, trying to keep his voice steady. "What do you want?"

The woman didn't speak. Instead, she lunged at them, her fingers gnarled and her teeth bared. Alex and Lila sprang into action, using their strength and agility to fight back.

But Tomas knew that brute force wouldn't be enough to defeat this woman. He closed his eyes and focused on his intuition. He felt the power surge through him, connecting him to the artifact they had found in the woods.

With a burst of energy, he harnessed the power of the artifact and banished the darkness from the woman. She stumbled back, confused and disoriented, before collapsing onto the ground.

Tomas and his friends stood panting, their hearts pounding with adrenaline. They had faced another obstacle, but they had come out victorious.

As they walked away from the clearing, Tomas knew that their journey wasn't over. The darkness was still out there, waiting for them. But he also knew that with his intuition and the power of the artifact, they had a fighting chance. They would continue on, always aware and always ready, because the power of intuition was the strongest weapon they had against the darkness.

Chapter 59

As they walked through the dense woods, Tomas couldn't shake
the feeling of unease that had settled over him. His
intuition was screaming at him to watch his back. He
scanned the dark trees, searching for any sign of danger. Suddenly, he heard a
twig snap
behind him and whirled around, his hand reaching for the artifact. But there
was nobody there.
Tomas's heart raced as he realized that his worst fears were coming true. The
darkness was still out there, lurking in the shadows, waiting for the perfect moment to strike.
He knew they had to be careful, but how could they protect themselves from
an enemy they couldn't see?
As they continued on their journey, Tomas racked his brain for a solution.
Suddenly, an idea struck him. It was risky, but it just might work.
He turned to his friends, his voice low and urgent. "We need to split up."
His friends looked at him in horror. "What? Why?"
"We need to cover more ground," Tomas explained. "If we're all together, we're
an easy target. But if we split up,
we can cover more territory and keep the darkness off guard."
His friends hesitated, but they could see the determination in Tomas's eyes.
They knew he was their best chance at survival.
"Okay," John said, nodding. "But how do we know where to go?" Tomas
smiled. "Trust me. My intuition won't let us down."
And with that, they split up, each journeying into the unknown darkness with
only their wits and Tomas's

intuition to guide them. As Tomas ventured deeper into the woods, he knew that the darkness was still out there,

waiting for him. But he also knew that with his intuition, he might just be able to beat it.

His heart thundered in his chest as he pushed forward, his senses on high alert. He felt like he was walking through a

nightmare,

every twig snap and rustling leaf making him jump. But he didn't stop. He couldn't stop. He had to keep moving, keep searching for the darkness's weak spot.

Hours passed, and Tomas began to feel like he was making progress. He felt like he was getting closer to the enemy, like he could almost taste victory. And then, suddenly, he saw it.

It was a small, glowing orb, pulsing with an otherworldly light. Tomas's heart leapt. He knew what it was. It was the darkness's weakness. It was the key to their victory.

With a burst of energy, Tomas lunged forward, snatching the orb from the air. He felt a surge of power coursing

through him as he clutched the orb in his hand. He knew that this was it. This was the moment they had been waiting for.

Tomas turned toward the darkness, his eyes blazing.

"Come and get me," he shouted. "I'm ready for you."

And as he stood there, waiting for the darkness to come, Tomas knew that he had the power of intuition on his side.

He knew that they just might have a chance against the darkness's overwhelming power.

But he couldn't help but wonder...was it enough?

Chapter 60

Tomas crept through the dark woods, his senses on high alert. Every rustle of leaves, every snap of a twig set his

heart racing. He knew they were getting close to the source of the darkness that had plagued them for months, and he could feel the tension in the air. As he walked, he muttered a string of incantations under his breath, tracing a intricate pattern in the air with his finger. Suddenly, the ground began to shake, and a deafening roar echoed through the trees. Tomas stumbled and fell to the ground,

his head slamming against a tree root.

He blinked, trying to clear his vision, and when it finally came into focus, he saw the source of the shaking and roar.

A massive creature, at least twenty feet tall, towered over him, its eyes blazing with an otherworldly light.

Tomas scrambled to his feet, reaching for the artifact he had used to defeat the twisted woman and the dangerous woman in the forest. He held it aloft, and a surge of power coursed through him.

With a fierce determination, Tomas launched himself at the creature, his intuition guiding every move. He danced around its massive feet, dodging its crushing blows and

lashing out with the artifact whenever he saw an opening.

It was a brutal fight, with Tomas taking hit after hit, but his intuition never failed him. He knew exactly when to strike, when to dodge, and when to retreat.

Finally, after what seemed like hours, the creature let out a final roar and fell to the ground, defeated. Tomas slumped to his knees, breathing heavily but feeling victorious.

With a deep sense of gratitude, Tomas thanked his intuition for guiding him through the fight. He knew that there would be more battles ahead, more darkness to vanquish, but with his intuition as his guide, he felt ready to face whatever lay ahead.

Chapter 61

Tomas wiped the sweat from his forehead as he made his way back to his friends. They had split up to cover more ground and find any signs of the darkness that still

L ingered in the woods. Tomas had been wandering for what felt like hours when he heard a blood- curdling scream in the distance. His heart racing, he sprinted towards the sound, his intuition telling him that his friends were in danger. As he approached, he saw a figure standing over one of his friends, a look of pure terror etched on their face. The figure was shrouded in darkness, but Tomas could see

glowing red eyes staring back at him. Without hesitation,

Tomas pulled out the magical artifact that they had found and began to chant the incantations he had learned. The creature hissed and lunged at Tomas, but he was too quick for it. His intuition had led him to the creature's weakness, and he struck it with the artifact, causing it to screech in agony. The creature disappeared into the darkness, leaving Tomas and his friends shaken and breathless. "What the hell was that?" one of his friends shouted as they helped the victim up. "I don't know," Tomas replied, "but we need to keep moving. There's still darkness here, and we need to get rid of it before it's too late." They continued on, their nerves on edge after the unexpected attack. Tomas's intuition was working overtime, and he could sense that danger was lurking around every corner. They walked for what felt like hours, the darkness pressing in on them from all sides.

Suddenly, they heard a rustling in the bushes ahead of them. Tomas held up a hand, signaling for his friends to stop. He could feel his intuition kicking in, warning him that something was terribly wrong. They waited, their hearts pounding in their chests, as the rustling grew louder and closer.

Without warning, a monstrous creature stepped out from the bushes. Its eyes glowed red, and its mouth was filled with razor- sharp teeth. Before they could even react, the creature lunged at them, its massive claws outstretched.

Tomas acted on instinct, using the magical artifact to defend his friends. He could feel his intuition guiding him, telling him the moment to strike. With a flash of brilliant light, the creature was gone, dissipating into the darkness like smoke.

Tomas and his friends stood there, stunned and shaken by the attack. They knew that there was still much work to be done before they could banish the darkness completely, but they also knew that they had a powerful weapon on their side: Tomas's intuition. With it, they would face whatever horrors lay ahead and emerge victorious.

Chapter 62

Tomas and his friends trudged through the thick underbrush of the woods, their hearts pounding with

anxiety. Despite their recent victories against the darkness, they could sense that they were still not safe.

Suddenly, Tomas dropped to his knees, clutching his head in agony. His friends rushed to his side, but he waved them away, gritting his teeth against the pain.

"I sense something," he gasped. "It's close."

The others tensed, their eyes scanning the woods for any sign of danger. A twig snapped in the distance, and they spun around, ready to face whatever came their way.

Out of the darkness stepped a figure, tall and lean, with piercing, malevolent eyes. Tomas recognized it immediately - it was the source of the darkness that had haunted him for so long.

"You have come far, Tomas," it hissed, its voice echoing through the woods. "But you cannot defeat me. I am too powerful."

Tomas stood, clutching the magical artifact tightly in his hand. He could feel the energy pulsing through it, warming his skin. With a fierce determination, he raised the artifact and began to chant.

The darkness snarled, its eyes burning with fury. It lunged forward, but Tomas was ready. He dodged its attacks,

weaving through the trees with fluid grace. The others watched in awe as he battled the darkness, his movements almost supernatural.

Finally, with a final burst of strength, Tomas sent a blast of energy straight into the heart of the darkness. It screamed

In agony, thrashing wildly before collapsing to the ground.

The group stood, panting and shaking, as the darkness slowly dissipated.

They had won the battle, but they knew the war was far from over.

"What now?" one of the others asked, breaking the silence.

Tomas just smiled grimly. "We keep going," he said. "We keep fighting, until the darkness is nothing but a

memory."

Chapter 63

Tomas and his friends stumbled out of the woods, exhausted and battered but victorious. They leaned against each other, gasping for breath, as they looked back at the trees that had been their battleground. Black smoke and darkness still lingered in the air, but it was slowly dissipating. They knew they had banished the malevolent presence from John's home and the woods, but they couldn't let their guard down yet.

"We need to find out who or what summoned that darkness," Tomas said, breaking the silence. "It didn't just appear out of thin air."

Michael nodded in agreement. "I'll do some research and see if I can find any information on powerful entities that could have done this."

Tomas's intuition tingled again, and he turned toward the direction of his family's home, feeling a pull he couldn't ignore. "I need to go home. I think there's something there I need to see."

His friends exchanged worried looks, but they knew better than to argue with Tomas's intuition. They drove him to his family's home, and Tomas hesitated before opening the door.

Inside, the house was eerily quiet. Tomas's heart pounded as he walked down the familiar hallway, his intuition on high alert. He stopped in front of a door that led to the basement, feeling a strong pull from within.

Without hesitation, Tomas opened the door and descended the stairs. The basement was dark, but Tomas's intuition guided him to a corner where a large chest sat. It was the same chest his grandfather had always warned him to stay away from, saying it contained dark magic and dangerous artifacts.

Tomas knew what he had to do. He opened the chest and found a book bound in human skin. It was a grimoire, a

book of spells and dark magic that had been passed down through his family for generations.

He paused for a moment, feeling a sense of responsibility and a strange connection to the book. He knew he had to

destroy it, but he couldn't just burn it or throw it away. He had to use his intuition to find the right way to destroy it, to ensure that the darkness it contained would never harm anyone again.

Tomas took the book and left the house, his friends following close behind. They drove to the nearest lake and Tomas walked to the edge, holding the book in his hands.

He closed his eyes, focusing his intuition, and threw the book into the water. As the book sank beneath the surface, Tomas felt a weight lift from his shoulders. He knew that the darkness that had plagued his family and those around him for generations

was finally gone. It was time to move forward and embrace the power of his intuition, using it to help others and protect them from the darkness that still lurked in the world.

Chapter 64

Tomas sat alone in his family's home, surrounded by the pieces of the grimoire he had destroyed. He couldn't believe what he had just done. Destroying a grimoire, a treasured book of spells and incantations passed down through generations of his family, had been unthinkable. But his intuition had led him there, and he knew it was the right thing to do.

As he sat and contemplated the destruction of the grimoire, he heard a soft knock at the door. Tomas rose from his seat and approached the threshold cautiously. He peered through the peephole and saw John standing outside, his face pale and his eyes wide with fear.

Tomas opened the door and greeted his friend warmly. "Is everything okay?" he asked.

John shook his head. "No, it's not," he said. "I think...I think something's following me."

Tomas's heart raced as he listened to John's story. He had banished the darkness from John's home, but he had a sinking feeling that it had found a way to return. He could feel the hairs on the back of his neck standing up as he thought about the malevolent force that had been haunting them.

He knew he had to act quickly. "Come inside," he said, beckoning John into the house. "We need to figure out what's going on."

Tomas led John to the living room and sat him down on the couch. He paced back and forth, his mind racing as he tried to come up with a plan. He couldn't let the darkness win. Not again.

Suddenly, Tomas's eyes flickered to a nearby bookshelf. He strode over to it and quickly scanned the rows of books.

And then he saw it: a small, tattered volume with a worn leather cover. It was an old book of charms and talismans, passed down from his grandmother.

Tomas reached out and took the book from the shelf. He flipped through the pages quickly, looking for anything that could help them. And then he saw it: a spell for banishing malevolent spirits.

With a sense of urgency, Tomas read the spell aloud. He spoke the words with confidence, feeling the power of the ancient magic flowing through him. He could feel the darkness retreating, shrinking away from the light of his intuition.

And then, suddenly, it was gone. The malevolent presence that had been following John vanished in an instant, leaving behind only a faint echo of its power.

Tomas collapsed onto the couch, exhausted but relieved. He looked over at John, who was staring at him with a mix of awe and gratitude.

"You did it," John said softly. "You banished it."

Tomas smiled weakly. "For now," he said. "But we have to be vigilant. We can't let it come back."

And with that, Tomas knew that his journey was far from over. The power of his intuition had saved them once again, but there were still mysteries to unravel, and darkness to banish. Tomas was ready for whatever lay ahead.

Chapter 65

Tomas spent the next few days studying the book of charms and talismans. He discovered that the banishing

spell he had used on John's malevolent spirit was just the

tip of the iceberg. There were countless other spells and incantations that could ward off evil and protect the innocent.

As he delved deeper into the book, Tomas felt a sense of unease creeping up on him. The more he learned, the more he realized just how dangerous the world he had stumbled into truly was. The darkness wasn't some intangible force

That he could simply banish with a few words and a wave of

his hand. It was a living, breathing entity that would stop

at nothing to destroy him and
everything he held dear.

Despite the fear that gnawed at his gut, Tomas knew he could never turn his back on the knowledge he had

uncovered. The grimoire he had destroyed was just the first step in a long and treacherous journey. There were other books out there, other artifacts and relics that could aid him in his quest.

So he gathered his friends once again, and they set out into the world, determined to find and destroy every last

vestige of darkness. They traveled far and wide, through forests and deserts, across oceans and mountains. They battled creatures beyond imagining, and faced death in a thousand different forms.

But through it all, Tomas kept his faith in his intuition, his unwavering belief that he had been chosen for this task for a reason. And in the end, it was that faith that saved them all, when they faced the darkness in its truest form, and Tomas knew just what spell to use to banish it back to the abyss from whence it came.

As they returned home, victorious but exhausted, Tomas knew that the world was still a dangerous place. But he also knew that, with his intuition guiding him, he and his

friends would never be caught off guard again. They had the power to protect themselves and others, and they would use it to keep darkness at bay for as long as they lived.

Chapter 66

Tomas and his friends had been on the road for weeks, traveling to remote locations to battle evil that had been
unleashed. Their intuition had guided them to each new destination, and their courage
had seen them through each fight. But as they traveled deeper into the heart of the forest, Tomas's intuition began to scream at him.

"We need to be careful," he said to his friends. "There's something here that's not quite right."

His friends looked at him skeptically, but they trusted
Tomas, and they knew that he would never lead them astray. As they continued to walk, their surroundings grew darker, and the trees seemed to loom over them like
menacing giants. A chill ran down Tomas's spine as he felt a cold breeze brush against his skin.

Suddenly, they heard a rustling in the bushes. Tomas reached for the magical artifact that he had used to defeat the darkness before, but it was gone. He cursed under his breath and looked around, searching for anything that could help them.

And then they saw it.

A figure emerged from the bushes, its eyes glowing with a malevolent hunger. It moved towards them, and Tomas
could feel its power radiating off of it like a heat wave. He knew that they were outmatched, but he refused to back
down. He stood his ground, and he called upon his newly honed intuition to guide him.

With a burst of energy, Tomas summoned a shield that protected him and his friends from the entity's attacks. He then called upon his friends to use their own magical
abilities to weaken the figure. Together, they unleashed a barrage of spells and charms, and slowly but surely, the entity began to weaken.
Finally, with one last burst of energy, Tomas struck the entity down, banishing it back to the darkness from
whence it came. He and his friends stood there, panting and sweating, but triumphant.
"We did it," Tomas said, a sense of pride filling him up.
"We banished the darkness again."
But even as he spoke, he knew that the fight was far from over. There would always be another entity, always another
darkness to vanquish. But with his intuition and his friends by his side, Tomas knew that they would always be ready to face whatever evil came their way.

Chapter 67

Despite banishing the malevolent entity, Tomas couldn't shake off the unease that had settled deep in his gut. His
intuition was screaming at him, warning him of a darkness far more powerful than anything they had ever
encountered before. He shared his concerns with his friends, who had grown to trust his instincts.
They searched for answers, scouring ancient texts and ancient burial sites. But they found nothing to put their

fears to rest. As they traveled deeper into the forest, they

were accosted by a new and terrifying presence. It was like nothing they had ever encountered before, and it seemed to be feeding on their fear.
Tomas tried to hold it at bay with his intuition, but it seemed to be growing stronger. His friends were no match for this new enemy, and it was only a matter of time before they were overpowered.
Tomas knew then what he had to do. He closed his eyes and focused all his energy on his intuition, summoning every
bit of strength he had. The power flowed through him like a river, and he felt himself connecting with the ancient forces of the universe.
Tomas opened his eyes and unleashed a blast of pure energy that obliterated the dark presence.
But as the dust settled, Tomas realized that he had paid a terrible price for his victory. He had unleashed something
far more sinister than anything they had ever faced before, and it was coming for them. And this time, they might not be strong enough to fight it.

Chapter 68

Tomas and his friends staggered back, panting and sweating, as the blinding flash of energy dissipated, leaving them temporarily deafened and disoriented. When they finally regained their bearings, they saw the shapeless thing writhing and thrashing on the ground, emitting a high-pitched whine that made their teeth ache.

"What the hell was that?" John shouted, his voice barely audible over the creature's keening.

"I don't know," Tomas snapped back, his nerves jangling. "But I don't think we've seen the last of it."

As if on cue, the thing suddenly vanished, leaving no traces behind. In the sudden silence that followed, Tomas became aware of a faint rustling in the nearby underbrush. He could sense a presence there, something or someone watching them. His intuition prickled, warning him of danger.

"Who's there?" he called out, his hand tightening around the hilt of his sword. There was no reply, only the rustling growing louder.

Tomas stepped forward, trying to get a better look. Suddenly, a figure emerged from the shadows, walking slowly towards them.

It was a woman, tall and slim, with hair as black as coal and eyes as green as emeralds. She wore a long, flowing gown made of shimmering silks, and carried a staff of carved wood that glowed with an inner light. Tomas could feel the power and the magic emanating from her like an aura.

"Who are you?" he asked, his voice low and cautious.

The woman smiled, revealing teeth as white as pearls. "I am called the Wander-er," she said, her voice deep and musical. "And I have been looking for you, Tomas." Tomas felt a shiver run down his spine. How did she know his name? Who was she? And why did he feel such an overwhelming sense of dread and respect in her presence?

"What do you want from me?" he asked, his hand still on his sword.

The Wanderer lifted her staff, and suddenly the forest around them changed. The trees grew taller and darker, their branches turning into skeletal claws. The ground beneath their feet turned to mud, and the sky above them became a writhing mass of dark clouds.

"I want to offer you a deal," she said, her eyes boring into his.

Tomas felt a sudden surge of fear and defiance. "I don't make deals with strangers," he said, stepping back.

The Wanderer chuckled, but the sound was like a thousand snakes hissing.

"You will," she said, pointing her staff at him. "Or you will regret it."

And with that, she vanished into thin air, leaving Tomas and his friends alone in the dark, twisted forest.

Chapter 69

Tomas stared at the Wanderer, trying to decide whether she posed as a greater threat than the forces of darkness they had already encountered. She smiled cryptically,
revealing sharp teeth, and beckoned him to follow her.
The forest was a twisted maze, and Tomas and his friends quickly lost their bearings. The trees were gnarled and

twisted, their branches reaching out like skeletal fingers.

The air was thick with an acrid scent, and the ground was cold and damp.
As they followed the Wanderer, Tomas felt a growing sense of unease. He had learned to trust his intuition, and it was
telling him
that they were walking into a trap. He signaled to his friends to keep their guard up, but they seemed oblivious to his warnings.
The Wanderer led them to a clearing, where a circle of stones glimmered dully in the moonlight. In the center of the circle was a
S tone altar, and on the altar rested a small, glowing object.
Tomas recognized it immediately – it was a talisman of immense power, one that could destroy the most powerful of dark entities.
The Wanderer gestured to the talisman. "This is what you seek," she said. "Take it and use it to defeat your enemies."
Tomas hesitated. Something about the Wanderer's words made him uneasy.
He sensed a hidden motive, a dark purpose lurking beneath her honeyed words.

As he reached out to take the talisman, he felt a sudden jolt of pain. It was as if a thousand needles were piercing his skin, a thousand voices screaming in his mind. He recoiled, gasping for breath.

The Wanderer laughed. "You are not as clever as you think, Tomas," she said. "You cannot defeat me with your intuition alone. You need me, and I will take what I want."

With that, she vanished into the darkness, leaving Tomas and his friends surrounded by an army of shadowy figures.

They had fallen right into her trap, and now they would have to fight for their lives.

Tomas gritted his teeth and called upon every ounce of his strength. He knew that they were outnumbered and outmatched, but he also knew that he had the power of intuition on his side. With a fierce determination, he plunged into the fray, ready to face whatever horrors came his way.

Chapter 70

Tomas and his friends stood back to back, surrounded by an army of shadowy figures. The air was thick with the
stench of death, and the sound of their ragged breathing echoed through the forest. The creatures closed in, their eyes glowing with an otherworldly light. Tomas gripped his talisman tightly, feeling its power pulsing through his veins. He closed his eyes and focused on his intuition, seeking any advantage he could find.

S uddenly, he felt a jolt of energy and opened his eyes to see a bright light emanating from the talisman. The creatures recoiled, their eyes shrinking away from the light.

"Get behind me!" Tomas shouted to his friends. "I'll shield us!"

Tomas extended his hand, and the light grew brighter, forming a barrier around him and his friends. The

creatures snarled and hissed, clawing at the barrier, but

they could not penetrate it. Tomas felt his energy draining, but he gritted his teeth and held on, determined not to let his friends down.

Suddenly, he heard a scream, and one of his friends was pulled away from the barrier by a shadowy figure. Tomas felt a surge of panic and anger, and the light around him exploded outward, blasting the creatures away from them.

"Run!" he shouted to his friends. "I'll hold them off!"

His friends fled into the forest, and Tomas stood alone, facing the army of shadowy figures. He felt a surge of fear, but he pushed it away, remembering all the times he had relied on his intuition to save him.

He closed his eyes and focused, feeling his intuition guiding him. Suddenly, he felt a jolt of energy and opened
his eyes to see a bright light emanating from his hands. He extended his arms and felt the energy surge forward, blasting through the creatures and scattering them like leaves in the wind.
Tomas stood panting and shaking, feeling the weight of his exhaustion and the terror of the battle. But he also felt a deep
sense of pride and accomplishment, knowing that he had faced his fears and triumphed.
He turned to follow his friends into the forest, but as he looked back, he saw a figure standing in the shadows. It was the Wanderer, watching him with a strange expression on her face.
Tomas felt a chill run down his spine, but he also felt a sense of curiosity and defiance. He lifted his talisman and pointed it at the Wanderer, feeling its power pulsing through him.

"You made a deal with me, but you betrayed us," he said.

"Now you will pay the price."
The Wanderer did not move or speak, but her eyes glinted in the darkness.
Tomas lowered his talisman and turned away, feeling a sense of satisfaction and finality.
He followed his friends into the forest, feeling the weight of the talisman in his hand and the power of his intuition in his heart. He did not know what lay ahead, but he knew that he was ready to face it, whatever it may be.

Chapter 71

As Tomas and his friends trudged through the dark and tangled forest, they stumbled across an ancient-looking

cabin. It was seemingly deserted, but there was something unsettling about it. Tomas felt his intuition kicking in again, this time telling him that something was not right.

They cautiously approached the cabin and peered through the dusty windows. Inside, they saw a woman sitting at a

table surrounded by various trinkets and potions. She had long, flowing black hair and wore an odd assortment of

clothing, which gave her an otherworldly appearance. She looked up and noticed them staring at her, beckoning them to come inside.

Tomas hesitated, but his friends were drawn to the woman's mysterious presence and they eagerly entered the cabin. The woman introduced herself as Zara, a self-

proclaimed expert in the field of dark magic. She claimed that she could help them defeat

the Wanderer and put an end to their nightmare.

Tomas was wary of Zara's intentions, but his friends were convinced that she could be the answer to their problems.

They were desperate for a way out of this horrid situation and were willing to try anything.

Zara told them that she needed a rare ingredient for her spell, one that could only be found deep in the heart of the forest. She offered to guide them to the location, but warned them of the dangers that lay ahead.

Tomas weighed the risks and benefits, his intuition telling him that Zara was not to be trusted. However, the allure of finding a solution to their problem was too great to resist and they followed Zara into the forest.

As they trekked further into the eerie woods, Tomas couldn't shake the feeling that they were being watched.

The air grew colder and the trees twisted and contorted into grotesque shapes. His heart raced as he felt a sense of impending doom.

Suddenly, they heard a bloodcurdling scream in the distance, and Zara stopped in her tracks. She whispered a curse under her breath and turned to Tomas and his friends with a sinister smile.

"Looks like we're not alone in these woods," she said, her eyes glinting with malice. "Be careful who you trust, my dears. You never know who might be lurking in the shadows."

Tomas felt a chill run down his spine as he realized that they had made a grave mistake in following Zara. He knew they were in deep trouble, and that their intuition might be the only thing that could save them now.

Chapter 72

Tomas and his friends sprinted towards the direction of the scream, following Zara's lead. The dense forest obscured their vision as they frantically looked for any sign of danger.

Suddenly, they found themselves in a clearing, surrounded by a group of hooded figures with torches in their hands. The figures' eyes glowed with an otherworldly aura as they chanted in unison, their voices echoing through the forest.

Tomas's intuition blared in his mind, warning him of the danger. He tried to pull his friends back but it was too late. The figures closed in on them, their movements fluid and eerie.

Just as Tomas thought that they were going to meet their end, something very surprising occurred. The hooded figures began to tremble and convulse, as if they were being controlled by an external force.

In a blinding flash, the hooded figures dissipated, leaving behind a trail of ash. Tomas and his friends stood there, dumbfounded.

Zara emerged from the shadows, her face devoid of any expression. "Well, that was unexpected," she remarked.

Tomas glared at her. "What did you do?"

"I didn't do anything," Zara said, defensively. "I think...I think someone else did."

Tomas's intuition flared again, this time with a sense of recognition. He closed his eyes and concentrated, trying to grasp at the source of the power that had just saved them.

When he opened his eyes, he saw a familiar figure standing in front of him. "Mom?" he whispered, in disbelief.

His mother smiled at him, her face radiant. "Hello, Tomas. It's been a long time."

Tomas's friends watched in awe as the woman embraced Tomas, tears streaming down their faces. Even Zara seemed to be affected, her face softening for a brief moment.

But Tomas's intuition nagged at him, warning him that there was something else at play. He pulled away from his mother, studying her features.

"Mom, how are you...here?" he asked, hesitantly.

His mother's smile faded, replaced by a look of grim determination. "It's a long story," she said, cryptically. "But right now, we need to focus on getting out of here alive."

Chapter 73

Tomas's heart was pounding as he followed his mother,

Claire, through the dense forest. He couldn't believe she had come to rescue them, but he also couldn't shake the feeling that something was off. They had been walking for almost an hour, and Tomas's intuition told him that they were being led somewhere.

Suddenly, Claire stopped in her tracks and turned to face them. "Listen carefully," she said, her voice low and urgent. "I came here to help you, but we're being followed. We need to move quickly."

Tomas felt a shiver run down his spine as he looked around, but all he could see was trees and bushes. "What do you mean we're being followed?" he asked.

Claire didn't answer. Instead, she began to walk again, this time at a faster pace. Tomas and his friends scrambled to keep up, their hearts racing with fear.

They had been walking for only a few minutes when they heard a sound behind them. Tomas turned and saw a group of hooded figures emerging from the trees.

"Run!" he yelled, grabbing his friends' arms and pulling them along.

They ran as fast as they could, but the figures were gaining on them. Tomas's heart was pounding so hard he thought it would burst out of his chest. He could hear his friends breathing heavily beside him, their footsteps echoing through the forest.

Suddenly, they reached a clearing, and Tomas's heart sank. In the center of the clearing was a stone altar, and standing beside it was Zara, holding a large, black book.

Tomas's intuition told him that they were in deep trouble, but he also knew that he couldn't let Zara get her hands on the talisman. He pulled it from his pocket and held it tight, feeling its power course through his body.

Zara began to chant, and Tomas felt a wave of dark energy wash over him. He could feel his strength beginning to fade, but he refused to let go of the talisman.

Suddenly, there was a blinding flash of light, and Tomas felt the ground shake beneath his feet. He opened his eyes and saw a figure standing in front of him, holding a glowing sword.

"Who are you?" Tomas asked, but he already knew the answer.

The figure turned to face him, and Tomas felt his heart skip a beat. It was the Wanderer.

"You don't belong here," the Wanderer said, his voice low and menacing.

Tomas felt a surge of anger and defiance rise up within him. "Neither do you," he said, his voice shaking with emotion.

The Wanderer raised his sword, and Tomas knew that the final battle had begun. He gripped the talisman tightly and prepared to face his greatest foe yet.

Chapter 74

Tomas took a deep breath as he stood in front of Zara and the Wanderer. The clearing was eerily silent except for the sound of their breathing. Tomas knew that this was the final battle, and he had to act quickly.

"You will never win," Zara spat, her eyes piercing through Tomas. "You and your friends will fall to the darkness, just like the others before you."

Tomas felt a chill run down his spine. He didn't want to admit it, but part of him knew that Zara was right. The odds were stacked against them, and the Wanderer's power was unlike anything he had ever seen.

But then, something inside him shifted. His intuition started to guide him, and he felt a surge of confidence build up inside him.

"Never say never," Tomas said, his voice surprisingly calm. "We have something that you don't."

"And what might that be?" Zara sneered.

"Each other," Tomas said, looking around at his friends. "We're together, and we won't let the darkness tear us apart."

The Wanderer let out a low growl, and Tomas could feel the ground shake beneath his feet. But then, something incredible happened. The trees around them started to glow, filling the clearing with a warm light. The hooded figures around them began to disintegrate, turning into dust and disappearing into the air.

Tomas looked around, stunned by what he was seeing. He knew that this wasn't his doing - it was something else, something greater.

Then, he saw her. Claire stood at the edge of the clearing, her arms outstretched, her eyes closed. She was surrounded by a glowing aura, and her presence was calming and protective.

Tomas realized that his mother had saved them once again. "Let's go," Tomas whispered to his friends, breaking the spell.

Together, they ran towards Claire, and the glowing aura expanded, enveloping them in a warm embrace. Tomas

K new that they weren't out of danger yet, but he also knew that they had the power of intuition on their side - and that was a force to be reckoned with.

Chapter 75

Tomas and his friends didn't dare stop, even when they were sure they had put enough distance between them and their enemies. They didn't know where they were going, but Claire urged them to keep moving, saying they were heading to a safe place.

As they trudged on, Tomas's intuition grew stronger, warning him that something was off. They had seen no signs of life since they entered the forest, but now Tomas was sure they were being followed.

Tomas whispered his suspicions to his friends, and they all went into high alert, scanning the surrounding woods for any signs of movement. But there was none, and they

continued on in silence, waiting for something to happen.

And then it did. Suddenly, a figure appeared in front of them, blocking their path. It was a woman, dressed in rags and twigs, her hair wild and unkempt. She didn't say a word, but her eyes narrowed menacingly as she looked them over.

Tomas felt his heart pounding in his chest as the woman began to move towards them, her movements jerky and unnatural. Alex and Lila instinctively stepped back, but

Tomas stood his ground, his intuition telling him that they needed to face this new threat head-on.

Just as the woman was about to attack, another figure emerged from the trees, an old man with a staff. Tomas saw recognition in his mother's eyes as she stepped forward to face him. The old man began to speak, his voice low and gravelly.

"You have meddled in things you do not understand. The spirits do not take kindly to those who interfere in their affairs. You must leave this place, or suffer the consequences."

Tomas tried to speak, but the old man held up his hand, cutting him off.

"I am not finished. You have already angered them, and they will not rest until they have their revenge. You must be prepared for what is to come."

With that, the old man disappeared back into the forest, leaving Tomas and his friends shaken and uncertain. They continued on, but Tomas couldn't shake the feeling that they were walking into something much darker than they had ever imagined.

Chapter 76

Tomas couldn't shake off the feeling of unease that had settled in his chest since they left the old couple. They seemed to know more than they were letting on, and their warning only added to his fear. He kept his eyes peeled for any signs of danger as they walked deeper into the forest.

As they walked, they stumbled upon a clearing, and Tomas froze in place. Something was off. The trees surrounding the clearing looked sickly, their leaves yellowing and falling off. The ground was barren and scorched. It was as if something had sucked all the life out of the area.

Suddenly, Tomas heard a deafening roar, and he felt his heart stop. The same sound they had heard on the road echoed through the clearing. He turned around, and his blood ran cold as he saw a pair of glowing red eyes in the distance.

Tomas's intuition told him to run, and he didn't hesitate to grab his friends and pull them towards the forest on the opposite side. As they ran, they heard the sound of footsteps getting closer and closer. They sprinted through the forest, branches slapping at their faces and arms as they weaved through the trees.

Finally, they burst out of the forest and into a small town.

They stumbled into a diner, panting and sweating. Tomas's intuition was still on high alert. He scanned the surroundings, but everything seemed normal. Until he saw a newspaper lying on the counter.

The headline read: "Massacre in the woods: Five hikers found dead."

Tomas's intuition had been right all along. They were in danger, and they needed to find a way out before it was too late.

Chapter 77

Despite the horrors they had faced, Tomas and his friends could not resist the pull of the supernatural. The
newspaper article detailing the massacre in the woods only made them more curious and determined to uncover the truth. They began to investigate, interviewing locals and poring over old books in the library.
But as they delved deeper into the mystery, strange things began to happen. Objects moved on their own, shadows
seemed to lurk around every corner, and Tomas couldn't shake the feeling that they were being watched. His
intuition told him that they were in danger, but his friends dismissed his warnings as paranoia.

One night, as they were in their motel room, a low growl
filled the air. The room grew icy cold, and they saw a dark

F igure slithering towards them. Tomas tried to scream, but
his voice was caught in his throat. The figure drew closer and closer, until
it was looming
over them.
Suddenly, Tomas's intuition kicked into overdrive. He closed his eyes and focused on his breathing, trying to calm
his racing heart. Slowly, he began to visualize a white light glowing around him, pushing back the darkness. The
figure shrieked and recoiled, as if burned by the light.
Tomas opened his eyes and saw that the figure had vanished. His friends
looked at him in awe, as if seeing him

in a new light. From that moment on, Tomas's intuition was stronger than ever. He knew that they were still in

danger, but he also knew that he had the power to protect them. They continued their investigation, determined to uncover the truth behind the massacre in the woods. But they also knew that they had to be careful, because the darkness was never far away.

Chapter 78

As they walked through the town, Tomas felt a sense of unease wash over him. The atmosphere was heavy and

Oppressive, and the air hung thick with the stench of decay. It felt like they were walking through a graveyard. They passed by an old abandoned mansion, the windows boarded up and the walls covered in ivy. Despite the

obvious signs of neglect, Tomas sensed that something

was still alive inside. He couldn't explain it, but he knew that they needed to investigate the mansion.

Tomas convinced his friends to accompany him, and they made their way towards the mansion. As they approached, they heard something rustling in the bushes. Tomas's instincts told him to stay back, but he couldn't shake the feeling that they needed to investigate.

They cautiously entered the mansion, the floorboards creaking beneath their feet. The air was thick with the scent of rot and decay, and Tomas's heart raced as he felt a cold breeze blow past

him. He knew that there was something in this house, and it wasn't human. As they made their way through the mansion, they came across a room that was frozen in time. The furniture was covered in dust, and the walls were plastered with old

photographs. But the photographs weren't of people. They were of something else entirely, something that sent chills down Tomas's spine.

He couldn't put his finger on it, but he knew that they had stumbled upon something ancient and malevolent. Something that had been waiting for them.

Tomas's intuition told him that they needed to leave, and fast. But as they turned to go, they found themselves facing the very thing they had been searching for. The embodiment of evil itself, staring back at them with glowing red eyes.

Tomas knew that they were in grave danger, and he knew that the only way to survive was to rely on his intuition. His instincts had gotten them this far, and he knew that they would get them out of this alive.

They stood their ground, ready to face whatever lay ahead, but they knew that they were in for the fight of their lives.

Chapter 79

Tomas could feel his heart pounding in his chest as they faced off against the ancient evil. The air around them
seemed to grow heavier, and it was difficult to breathe.
He could see the figure of the evil lurking in the shadows, a twisted creature
that seemed to be made of pure darkness.
It let out a guttural growl that echoed through the mansion, shaking the old
walls.
Alex and Lila stood beside Tomas, their eyes wide with fear, but Tomas felt his
intuition kicking in once again. He knew that they
had to be calm and collected if they wanted to survive this encounter.
He took a deep breath and stepped forward, holding out his hands in a gesture
of peace. "We don't want to fight you," he said calmly. "We just want to know
what you want."
The creature snarled in response, and Tomas felt a sense of unease creeping
over him. He knew that this was not going to be an easy negotiation.
They started to back away, but the creature lunged forward, snatching Lila in
its claws. She screamed in terror as the creature began to drag her away.
Tomas felt his heart racing as he sprang into action, grabbing a nearby piece of
wood and swinging it with all his might. The makeshift weapon connected
with the creature, and it let out a roar of pain.
Alex joined in, grabbing another piece of wood and swinging it at the creature's head. Lila managed to wriggle free from its grip, and the three of them
ran towards the door.

As they burst out into the night air, Tomas could feel his adrenaline pumping. They had faced the ancient evil and lived to tell the tale, but he knew that this was just the beginning.

They had a long road ahead of them, and they would need to rely on each other and their intuition if they were going to succeed. Tomas took a deep breath and felt a sense of determination washing over him. Whatever was coming next, he was ready.

Chapter 80

As they made their way back to their car, Tomas couldn't shake the feeling that they were being watched. He glanced around nervously, but saw no signs of danger. Suddenly, Alex let out a loud fart, causing Lila to burst out laughing.

"Alex, that was disgusting!" Lila exclaimed, still giggling.

Tomas couldn't help but laugh along with them, feeling a wave of relief wash over him. For a moment, they had forgotten about the evil they had just faced and were simply three friends enjoying each other's company.
As they climbed into the car, Tomas couldn't help but feel grateful for their friendship and the sense of humor that had gotten them through so many tough situations.
"Well, that was certainly one way to break the tension," Tomas said, chuckling.
Alex grinned. "Hey, I'm just trying to keep things interesting."
Lila rolled her eyes but smiled. "Well, I think we can all agree that things are plenty interesting without your help." Tomas laughed again, feeling a sense of camaraderie with his friends. Despite the horrors they had faced, they were still able to find joy in the little moments.
As they pulled out of the driveway and headed back to their hotel, Tomas couldn't help but feel hopeful. They may be
facing an ancient evil, but with their intuition and their ability to make each other laugh, he knew they could overcome anything.

Chapter 81

As they drove away from the abandoned mansion, Tomas couldn't shake the feeling that they were being followed.

He glanced over his shoulder several times but saw nothing but darkness. Alex and Lila were talking and laughing in the front, oblivious to his unease.

Finally, Tomas spoke up. "Does anyone else feel like we're being watched?"

Lila turned around in her seat. "What do you mean?"

"I don't know. It's just a feeling. Like something is following us."

Alex scoffed. "Come on, man. We just fought an ancient evil. You think something is going to scare us now?"

Tomas shook his head. "I'm not scared. But we should still be careful."

They continued driving in silence, each lost in their own thoughts. Suddenly, the car jolted and swerved.

"What the hell?" Alex yelled as he fought to regain control. "Someone just hit us!"

The car spun out of control, coming to a stop in a ditch on the side of the road. Tomas was the first to open his door and stumble out into the night.

That's when he saw them. Three figures, silhouetted by the moonlight. They were tall and thin, with glowing yellow eyes that seemed to pierce through the darkness.

Tomas knew immediately that they weren't human. They were something far more dangerous.

He didn't hesitate. He reached into his pocket and pulled out a small vial of holy water. With a quick prayer, he flung it at the creatures. It exploded on impact, sending them screeching into the night.

Alex and Lila stumbled out of the car, looking around in confusion. "What the hell was that?" Lila asked.

"Demons," Tomas replied grimly. "They're after us."

Alex shook his head. "We can't keep running from this. We need to face them head-on."

Tomas nodded in agreement. "But we have to be careful.

We don't know what we're dealing with." He paused, then added. "And we need to find out who sent them after us."

The three of them got back in the car, ready to face whatever came their way. But Tomas knew that their battle against evil was far from over. And he couldn't shake the feeling that they were being watched, even as they drove away into the night.

Chapter 82

The car spun out of control as the demon-like creatures relentlessly chased them. Tomas held on tight to the steering wheel as Alex and Lila screamed in terror. They had trained for this moment, but nothing could prepare them for the reality of the situation. Tomas tried to shake off the creatures by driving through narrow alleys and backstreets, but they were always just a step behind. Suddenly, a giant beast appeared in front of them, blocking their path. The creature resembled a cross between a wolf and a reptile, with razor-sharp teeth and glowing red eyes.

Tomas instinctively slammed on the brakes, but the car skidded towards the creature, seemingly destined to crash into it. At the last moment, Tomas swerved the car to the left and sped past the creature. They narrowly avoided a collision, but the chase wasn't over yet.

The creatures continued to chase them, and the group reached a dead end. Tomas quickly reversed the car, narrowly avoiding the creatures as they charged towards them. The car screeched to a halt, and the team jumped out, ready to face their attackers. Tomas took out his weapons - a silver dagger and a small vial of holy water. Alex and Lila stood behind him, each holding a flashlight. The creatures surrounded them, growling and snarling like wild animals.

Tomas closed his eyes and concentrated, summoning all his courage and intuition. He could sense the evil radiating from the creatures, but he also sensed something else. He felt a faint glimmer of hope, as if some higher power was watching over them.

With a sudden burst of energy, Tomas lunged towards the creatures, striking out with his silver dagger. The creatures snarled and snapped at him, but Tomas was too quick for them. He dodged and weaved, slashing and stabbing with his dagger.

Alex and Lila used their flashlights to distract the creatures, blinding them with bright beams of light. The creatures screeched in pain, writhing and flailing in the darkness.

In the end, the team emerged victorious. The creatures vanished into thin air, leaving the group alone and trembling in the night. Tomas felt a sense of relief and triumph, but he also knew that they still had a long way to go.

As they walked back to their car, Tomas sensed something lurking in the shadows. He looked up at the sky, feeling a chill run down his spine. The stars seemed to be flickering, as if some cosmic force was watching over them.

Tomas knew that he and his friends were not alone in their battle against evil. They had the power of intuition on their side, and that was a force to be reckoned with.

Chapter 83

Tomas, Alex, and Lila drove through the night, exhausted from their intense battle with the demon-like creatures.

The car was damaged and they were running low on weapons and supplies. As they drove down a dark, deserted road, they suddenly spotted a sign that read "Welcome to the Haunted Forest." Tomas felt a chill run down his spine. He had heard legends of this forest but had never been brave enough to explore it. The stories told of ghosts, demons, and other supernatural creatures that roamed the forest, preying on unsuspecting travelers.

Alex scoffed at the sign, saying it was probably just a tourist trap. Lila, however, seemed intrigued by the idea of exploring the forest and suggested they stop and investigate.

Despite his reservations, Tomas knew that they needed to keep moving and find a safe place to rest. He reluctantly agreed, and they turned down a dirt road that led into the heart of the forest.

As they drove deeper into the woods, the darkness seemed to press in around them, and the trees loomed like silent sentinels.

Suddenly, the car sputtered and died, leaving them stranded in the middle of the forest.

Tomas tried to start the car again, but it refused to turn over. Alex and Lila glanced nervously at each other, realizing they were completely cut off from civilization.

As they stepped out of the car, a cold breeze rustled through the trees, and the sound of branches snapping echoed through the forest.

Tomas felt a tingling sensation in the back of his neck, warning him that danger was near. He reached into his bag and pulled out a flashlight and a silver cross, ready to defend himself and his friends.

As they made their way deeper into the forest, they stumbled upon an abandoned cabin. The door was ajar, and a flickering candle burned in the window.

Tomas led the way, cautiously entering the cabin. The walls were lined with shelves, filled with dusty tomes and strange artifacts.

As they explored the cabin, they heard a creaking noise upstairs. Tomas motioned for Alex and Lila to follow him as they climbed the stairs, weapons at the ready.

What they found at the top of the stairs made their blood run cold. A figure, shrouded in darkness, stood in front of them. Its eyes glowed with a sinister energy, and its hands curled into claws.

Tomas knew that this was the ancient evil they had encountered before. He raised his cross, calling upon the power of intuition and faith, and prepared to do battle once again.

Chapter 84

Tomas could feel his heart rate quicken as he entered the abandoned cabin.
The floorboards creaked beneath his
feet, and the air was thick with dust. Dark shadows danced on the walls, and
he could feel the hairs on his arms
standing on end. The others followed closely behind, their flashlights illuminating their path. Suddenly, a loud crash
startled them. The group spun around to find that the door had slammed shut
on its own.

Alex's voice broke the silence, "What the hell was that?"

Tomas took a deep breath, "I don't know, but we need to keep moving."
They continued down the hallway, their flashlights casting eerie shadows on
the walls. The air grew colder, and the
hairs on Tomas' arms stood on end once again. Suddenly, he could feel a presence behind him, lurking just out of
sight. He turned around, but there was nothing there.
Lila gasped, "Did you feel that?"
Tomas nodded, "Yeah, we need to keep moving."
As they turned the corner, a figure appeared before them. It was tall and gaunt,
with piercing red eyes. Its nails were long and twisted, and its skin was ashen.
Tomas spoke with authority, "Who are you?"
The figure grinned wickedly, "I am the ancient evil that lurks within these
woods. You have trespassed into my domain, and now you shall suffer the con-
sequences."
Tomas gripped his flashlight tightly, "We won't let you harm us."

With a piercing scream, the creature lunged at them. The trio fought with all
their might, striking it with their
weapons and flashing their lights in its face. Finally, the creature let out a loud
screech and vanished.
The group stood in silence, their hearts pounding in their chests. Tomas broke
the silence, "We need to leave this place, now."
As they made their way out of the cabin, they could feel the presence fading
away. The sun was just beginning to rise, casting a warm glow over the forest.
The group got into their car and drove away, exhausted but victorious.
Tomas glanced out the window, "We may have won this battle, but the war
against evil is far from over."

Chapter 85

Tomas felt uneasy as they left the Haunted Forest and returned to their car. He couldn't shake the feeling that
they were being followed, but he pushed it to the back of his mind. They needed to find a place to rest for the night.
As they drove down a deserted road, Lila suddenly screamed. Tomas slammed on the brakes, and they all turned to see what had caused her outburst.
Standing in the middle of the road was a figure dressed in tattered robes. Its face was obscured by a hood, and it held a staff adorned with strange symbols. Tomas and his friends sat frozen, watching as the figure approached their car. Tomas's intuition told him that this was no ordinary person. This was something ancient and powerful.

As the figure reached the car, it raised its staff and began to chant in a language that none of them understood. The air around them grew thick and oppressive, and Tomas felt his heart racing.
Suddenly, the figure stopped chanting and turned to stare directly at Tomas. For a moment, they locked eyes, and
Tomas felt a surge of fear wash over him. He knew that this creature could destroy them all without a second thought.
But as quickly as it had appeared, the figure turned and disappeared into the darkness. Tomas and his friends sat in stunned silence for several long minutes before Tomas finally spoke.
"We need to keep moving," he said, his voice barely above a whisper. "Whatever that was, it's not something we want to deal with."

The group got back into the car and drove off, the image of the mysterious figure burned into their minds. Tomas knew that their battle against evil had just taken a terrifying turn, and he wasn't sure if they were ready for what lay ahead. As they drove into the night, the looming threat of the figure and the ancient evil they had encountered in the

Haunted Forest hung heavily over them. Tomas could only hope that his intuition would guide them through the darkness and keep them safe from harm.

Chapter 86

Tomas and his friends were left reeling from their encounter with

the mysterious figure on the deserted road. They couldn't

shake off the feeling that they were being watched, even as they drove away from the spot where the figure had vanished.

As they made their way through the winding roads, Alex suddenly slammed on the brakes. "Look!" he exclaimed, pointing to a sign on the side of the road. Tomas peered through the windshield and saw that they had arrived at the town of Elmwood, known for its eerie

history and supernatural occurrences. He felt a shiver run down his spine as memories of his childhood dreams and nightmares about Elmwood flooded back to him.

"We should stop and take a look around," Lila suggested.

Tomas hesitated, but his intuition told him that they needed to explore Elmwood if they were to uncover the

truth about the dark forces that were after them. They pulled into a parking lot and set out on foot, their flashlights illuminating the deserted streets of the town.

As they walked, they heard a strange sound coming from an old abandoned house. Tomas felt drawn to investigate

and motioned for his friends to follow him. They cautiously approached the house and peered through a window, gasping in horror at what they saw inside.

A group of people dressed in black robes were performing a ritual, their faces obscured by hoods and masks. A young woman was tied to an altar in the center of the room, her eyes wide with terror.

Tomas knew that they had to intervene. He took a deep breath and kicked open the door, surprising the cultists and causing them to scatter. He rushed to untie the woman, but as he did so, he felt a sharp pain in his side.

One of the cultists had plunged a knife into his flesh, and

Tomas

fell to the floor, gasping for breath. He saw his friends rush to his side, but the darkness consumed him, and he felt himself slipping away.

As his vision grew dim and his consciousness faded, Tomas wondered if his intuition had led him and his friends to their doom.

Chapter 87

Tomas woke up in a strange room, surrounded by unfamiliar faces. Panic set in as he realized he couldn't

move his arms or legs. Looking down, he saw that he was

Strapped to a table and hooked up to various monitors and machines. Fear filled him as he tried to scream for help, but realized there was a tube down his throat.

Suddenly, a man in a lab coat entered the room. "Ah, you're awake," he said in a monotone voice. "I see the sedative we used worked well. Don't worry, you won't feel a thing."

Tomas struggled against his restraints as the man reached for a large needle. "What are you doing to me?" he managed to choke out.

"We are simply conducting an experiment," the man replied, injecting the needle into Tomas's arm. "We want to study the power of intuition, and you have proven to be a very interesting subject."

Tomas felt a surge of pain and then everything went black.

When he woke up again, he was back in the cabin with Alex and Lila, and everything seemed normal. But as the days

passed, Tomas couldn't shake the feeling that something was off. He couldn't trust his intuition anymore, and he feared what the scientists had done to him.

One night, as they sat around the fire, Tomas confided in

his friends about what had happened to him. Alex and Lila

were horrified, and they vowed to help Tomas find a way to
undo the damage. But as they dug deeper into the mystery, they realized
that the scientists were just pawns in a much larger, more sinister game.
Tomas's intuition had led them all into a trap, and now they were fighting for
their lives against a dark force that
was beyond their understanding. As they huddled together in the darkness,
they knew that they had to use their wits and their courage if they had any
hope of surviving. The
power of intuition may have led them into danger, but it would also be their
only hope for escaping it.

Chapter 88

Tomas sat in a cold, sterile room, his mind racing. He couldn't believe that he and his friends had fallen victim to a group of scientists who were experimenting on their intuition. He had always trusted his gut instincts, but now he was doubting everything.

As Tomas tried to free himself from the restraints on the table, he heard a voice echoing through the room. It was a woman's voice, soft and soothing, yet ominous.

"Tomas, we know you possess a unique ability," the voice said. "We are conducting experiments to tap into the power of intuition, to see if it can be harnessed to control the world."

Tomas tried to ignore the voice and concentrate on freeing himself, but his intuition was telling him that there was something else going on. He looked around the room, trying to identify the source of the voice.

Suddenly, a dark figure appeared in front of him. It was the same mysterious figure that had chanted in an unknown language back on the deserted road. The figure spoke to Tomas in that same language, and he felt a surge of fear rising in his chest. As the figure approached him, Tomas closed his eyes and focused all of his energy on his intuition. He could feel the power surging through him, and he knew that he had to use it to defeat this dark force.

With a burst of energy, Tomas broke free from the restraints and charged towards the figure. He could feel his friends joining him in the fight, and together they battled against the dark presence.

As the creature dissipated into the ether, Tomas and his friends were left standing in a state of shock. They knew
that their battle against evil had taken a dangerous turn, and they weren't sure what lay ahead.

Tomas looked at his friends, determination etched on his face.

"We can't give up," he said. "We have to keep fighting and trust our intuition. It's the only way we can defeat this
darkness."

Chapter 89

Tomas and his friends were now back on the road, hoping to escape the horrors that had become their reality. But just
as they thought they were in the clear, the car started to sputter and they pulled over to the side of the deserted road.

"Great, just what we needed. A broken-down car in the middle of nowhere," John muttered, clearly agitated.

Tomas surveyed their surroundings and couldn't shake the feeling that they were being watched. It was almost as if

the very trees were alive and watching their every move.

Suddenly, a loud growl erupted from the nearby woods, causing the group to jump with fear. They then saw a pair of glowing eyes staring at them from the darkness, and they realized they were not alone.

Without hesitation, Tomas pulled out his flashlight and shined it towards their attacker. But as he did, the creature lunged towards them, revealing its elongated claws and razor-sharp teeth.

Tomas acted on instinct, dodging the creature's attack and grabbing a nearby stick as a weapon. The rest of the group followed suit, using whatever they could find as makeshift weapons.

Their opponent was ferocious, but Tomas and his friends fought with everything they had. They relied on their
intuition to anticipate the creature's next move and strike when the opportunity presented itself.

After what felt like an eternity, the creature finally retreated back into the woods, leaving the group battered and shaken. But they were alive, and they had once again used their intuition to survive.

As they continued their journey, Tomas couldn't help but wonder what other horrors lay ahead. But he knew one

thing for sure: they were in this fight together, and they would use their intuition to overcome anything that came their way.

Chapter 90

Despite surviving the creature attack, Tomas and his friends were in bad shape. Lila had a deep gash on her leg, Alex's arm was badly bruised, and Tomas felt a sharp pain in his side every time he breathed. They knew they had to find help soon, but their options were limited on the deserted road.

As they stumbled down the road, Tomas's intuition began to nag at him. He felt like they were being watched, like something was following them. He tried to shake it off, thinking it was just his fear and exhaustion playing tricks on him.

But then, they heard a low growl, and Tomas's heart sank. He knew that sound. It was the creature's growl. They turned around and saw it, standing on its hind legs, its glowing eyes fixed on them. Tomas's intuition kicked into high gear. He knew they couldn't fight the creature again, not in their current state. They had to run, but where? There were no buildings or shelters in sight.

Lila let out a cry as she stumbled, and the creature lunged forward. Tomas reacted on instinct, grabbing Alex and Lila and pulling them behind him. He raised his makeshift weapon, a branch with a sharpened end, and braced for impact.

But then, something strange happened. The creature stopped inches away from them, its eyes flickering with confusion. Tomas felt a strange energy buzzing through him, like a force field pushing the creature back.

He looked at his friends, and they all had the same expression of shock and wonder on their faces. They had never seen anything like it.

As they continued down the road, Tomas couldn't shake the feeling that something had changed. They were no
longer just fighting for survival; they were fighting for something greater.
Something that had the power to
protect them and push back against the darkness.
Tomas knew that their intuition had brought them this far, and he had a feeling it would guide them to their next step.
But he also knew that the darkness was still out there, waiting for its next
move. And this time, they had to be ready.

Chapter 91

Tomas couldn't shake the feeling that something was watching them. He'd felt it since they left the deserted

road, and it had only intensified since they set up camp.

The hairs on his arms and the back of his neck stood on end as he listened to the rustling in the bushes around them.

Alex and Lila were asleep, but Tomas couldn't. He kept his eyes trained on the darkness that surrounded them.

It was the sound of a twig snapping that finally pushed Tomas over the edge. He sat up, grabbing the stick he'd been using as a

weapon. That's when he saw it.

There, on the edge of their campsite, stood a figure. It was tall, with elongated claws and razor-sharp teeth, just like the creature that had attacked them on the road. But this one was different. Its eyes glowed a sickly green, and its skin looked as though it was made of shadows. It was the most terrifying thing Tomas had ever seen.

He held his makeshift weapon tight and stood up, ready to fight. But the figure didn't move. It just stood there, watching them.

Tomas felt a strange energy building in his chest. It was like nothing he'd ever felt before. It was a power that came from somewhere deep within him, and he knew

instinctively that it was his intuition. He took a step forward, and the figure flinched.

Tomas began to move forward slowly, his eyes locked on the creature. The closer he got, the more he could feel the energy growing inside him. It was like he was tapping into something primal, something ancient.

The creature backed away, its shadowy form shifting and warping as it did so. It was like it was afraid of Tomas. And for the first time since they'd started this journey, Tomas felt a sense of victory. He had used his intuition to defeat this creature, just like he had used it to defeat the shadowy figure in the laboratory. But he knew that this was just the beginning. There were forces beyond his understanding that were working against him and his friends. And he was determined to use his intuition to defeat them all.

Chapter 92

Tomas woke up with a start, his heart pounding in his chest. He had been in the middle of a nightmare, but he couldn't remember what it was about. He looked around the dimly lit room, trying to orient himself.

Lila was snoring softly in the bed next to him, while Alex was curled up on the floor, using his backpack as a pillow.

Tomas got up and went to the window, pulling aside the curtains to look out. It was still dark outside, with only a sliver of a moon visible in the sky. The trees rustled in the wind, making eerie creaking sounds. Tomas felt a shiver run through him, and he rubbed his arms to warm himself up.

He turned away from the window and walked over to where Alex was sleeping. He nudged his friend gently, trying not to startle him awake.

"Alex," he whispered. "Wake up. We need to talk."

Alex stirred, rubbing his eyes. "What's up?" he asked groggily.

"I had a dream," Tomas said, keeping his voice low. "I don't remember what it was about, but it felt... important."

Alex sat up, looking concerned. "Do you think it was a warning?"

Tomas nodded. "Maybe. I just have a feeling that something's coming, and we need to be ready for it."

Lila stirred in her sleep, and the two men fell silent, not wanting to wake her up. They sat there in the dark, listening to the sounds of the forest outside.

It was a long night, filled with unease and uncertainty. But

Tomas felt a sense of purpose stirring within him, a conviction that he was meant to fight against the darkness and protect his friends.

As the first light of dawn began to filter through the window, he made a silent vow to himself: he would keep using his intuition to guide him, no matter what horrors lay ahead.

Chapter 93

With each passing day, Tomas felt a sense of relief wash over him. The darkness that had been plaguing his
thoughts and dreams seemed to dissipate, replaced by a newfound sense of hope. Maybe it was the crisp autumn air, or the warm sun on his face, but he felt better than he had in weeks.
He spent his days with Alex and Lila, exploring the surrounding countryside and searching for clues about the malevolent presence that had haunted them for so long.
They laughed and joked, and even though they all knew they were in danger, the weight of their burden felt a little lighter.
Tomas' intuition had always been a powerful force in his life, but he had never felt more attuned to it than he did
N ow. He could sense when danger was near, but he was also
able to recognize when it was safe to let his guard down.

For the first time in a long while, he felt like they were winning the battle against the darkness.
One day, they stumbled upon a small village nestled in a valley. The locals were friendly and welcoming, and they
spent hours chatting and sharing stories. Tomas couldn't help but notice how different this place felt compared to the other places they had visited. There was a sense of
peace and tranquility that permeated the air, and he found himself relaxing in a way he hadn't been able to in months.

As they left the village and started on the long journey home, Tomas couldn't help but smile. They had come so

far, seen so much, and yet he knew there was still more to

discover. But for the first time in a long time, he felt like they were up to the challenge. They had each
other, and they had their intuition, and that was all they needed to face whatever lay ahead.

Chapter 94

Tomas, Alex, and Lila had been traveling for days without encountering any more supernatural forces. They were
starting to
believe that their struggles were finally over and they could relax for a moment. They arrived at the friendly village that Tomas had sensed and were greeted warmly by the locals.
The villagers showed them around, offering food and shelter, and Tomas felt grateful for the hospitality.
As they were settling in for the night, a loud banging on the door startled them all. Tomas cautiously opened the door, only to be faced with a horrifying sight. The villagers they had just met were huddled outside, their faces twisted in

Fear, and their bodies covered in scratches and bite marks. Tomas recognized the marks as the same ones from the creature they had encountered before.
The villagers begged for help, explaining that a dark force had taken over their village, and they were the only ones
left. Tomas knew that they couldn't ignore their cries for help, so he rallied Alex and Lila, and they set out into the night to confront the evil that had taken over the village.
As they approached the village, they could feel the darkness closing in around them. Tomas' intuition was on
high alert, and he knew they were facing a powerful entity.
They found themselves surrounded by a horde of twisted, demonic creatures, and Tomas knew they had a fight on their hands.

Tomas fought with all his might, drawing on his intuition to predict the movements of the creatures and coordinate
his attacks with Alex and Lila. The battle raged on for what felt like hours, with Tomas and his companions barely managing to hold their own against the overwhelming odds.

Eventually, they emerged victorious, the last of the demonic creatures vanishing into the night. The villagers were all saved, and they cheered as they saw the trio's victory.

Tomas felt both relieved and unsettled. He knew that this was just one battle in a larger war against the darkness that
was trying to take over their world. But for now, he could take solace in the fact
that they had won this fight. Tomas had proven to himself that his intuition was a true power, and he would need to use it again in the battles that lay ahead.

Chapter 95

Tomas couldn't shake the feeling of unease that had settled over him since they left the village. The streets were empty, and the buildings were dark and silent. It was as if the village had been abandoned just moments before they arrived. Something was wrong, and Tomas knew it.

As they walked deeper into the village, they heard a low growling sound coming from one of the houses. Tomas

Motioned for Alex and Lila to follow him towards the noise. They approached the house cautiously, weapons drawn, ready for whatever lay ahead.

As they opened the door, they were immediately met with a putrid smell that made Lila gag. Inside, they found a gruesome scene: the bodies of villagers, torn apart and left in grotesque positions.

Tomas felt his stomach turn as his intuition told him that they weren't alone in the village. The hairs on the back of his neck stood up as he felt the presence of something watching them, something malevolent.

Suddenly, they heard a screeching sound from outside.

They rushed out of the house and saw a group of creatures with razor- sharp teeth and blood-red eyes, charging towards them.

Tomas and his companions fought with all their might, but they were outnumbered. They tried to retreat, but the creatures were too fast. Just when they thought all was lost, a bright light enveloped the village, and the creatures vanished.

Tomas looked around, trying to make sense of what had just happened. He felt relieved, but also terrified. They had won the battle, but the war was far from over. Tomas knew that they couldn't let their guard down, not even for a moment.

As they walked away from the village, Tomas felt his intuition guiding him once again. He knew that they had to find the source of the darkness and destroy it if they were to have any hope of winning this war.

Tomas, Alex, and Lila walked into the darkness, ready for whatever lay ahead. They knew that the power of their intuition was their best weapon, and they were determined to use it to defeat the darkness once and for all.

Chapter 96

As Tomas and his companions continued their journey, they couldn't shake off the feeling of unease that lingered within them. They traveled for days until they stumbled

upon a long-abandoned mansion on top of a hill. Tomas'

intuition sent alarm bells ringing in his mind, warning him to stay away. But, they all felt a strange pull towards the foreboding structure, a nagging curiosity that wouldn't let them leave.

As they entered the mansion, the air became thick with a strange energy, a tension that made their skin crawl. Every

S tep they took, the atmosphere seemed to grow thicker and more oppressive. Lila began to feel nauseous, and Alex's hands shook with fear. But Tomas, with his natural intuition, knew that they could not turn back.

They climbed the stairs to the upper floor, where a strange chanting echoed through the halls. And then they saw it - a circle of cloaked figures, standing in the center of the room, chanting in unison and holding an ornate box identical to the one they had found before.

Tomas knew what was happening. These people were attempting to summon dark forces into the world. But it

was too late, they had

already succeeded. A dark mist swept through the room, filling the air with the stench of decay and death. The cloaked figures turned towards the three companions, their eyes a deep, inky

black.

And then Tomas saw something that made his heart stop among the cloaked
figures stood a familiar face. It was
John, his friend. The fear and agony in his eyes sent a chill down Tomas' spine.
John, who had always been skeptical of the supernatural, had somehow become a part of it all.
Before Tomas could react, one of the cloaked figures lunged at them, intent on
sacrificing them to the dark
forces they had summoned. It was an all-out fight for
survival as the three companions fought their way through the cloaked figures,
racing against time to escape the
mansion and banish the darkness that had taken hold.
As they fled, with the sounds of the cloaked figures' screams echoing in their
ears, Tomas knew that they were
in for a long and difficult journey. The darkness had grown stronger, and they
had to find a way to destroy it before it consumed everything they held dear.

Chapter 97

Tomas, Alex, and Lila had been wandering aimlessly for hours, trying to find their way out of the dense forest surrounding the abandoned mansion. The sun was beginning to set, casting long shadows across the forest floor. Tomas's intuition was on high alert, warning him that danger was lurking nearby.

Suddenly, a piercing scream shattered the tranquility of the forest, causing the trio to freeze in their tracks. They exchanged worried glances before sprinting towards the direction of the scream.

As they pushed their way through the dense foliage, they saw a horrifying sight. A woman was being dragged by a group of grotesque creatures towards a nearby cave. Tomas recognized the creatures immediately - they were the same ones they had fought in the abandoned village.

Without hesitation, the trio charged towards the creatures. The battle was brutal and intense - both sides fought fiercely, neither willing to give an inch. Tomas used his intuition to anticipate the creatures' movements, dodging their attacks with ease. Alex and Lila fought with equal ferocity, taking out as many of the creatures as they could.

At last, the creatures began to retreat, slinking back into the shadows. The woman, battered and bruised, lay on the ground, gasping for breath.

Tomas knelt beside her, offering her a hand. "Are you okay?" he asked, concern etched on his face.

The woman nodded weakly, tears streaming down her face.

"Thank you," she whispered. "Thank you for saving me."

As they helped the woman to her feet, Tomas couldn't help but feel a sense of unease. There was something about the woman's demeanor that seemed off - her eyes were too bright, her movements too jerky.

Suddenly, the woman lunged at Tomas, her eyes blazing with an otherworldly light. He barely had time to react as she sank her teeth into his neck, her grip iron-tight.

Pain shot through Tomas's body as he struggled to free himself from the woman's grasp. Alex and Lila fought valiantly, but they were no match for the woman's strength.

It was only when Tomas's intuition kicked in that he realized the truth - the woman was possessed by the very darkness they had been fighting all along.

With a fierce determination, Tomas summoned all his strength and broke free of the woman's grip. He grabbed the ornate box they had been carrying and held it aloft, unleashing a powerful wave of light that banished the darkness.

As the light faded, Tomas collapsed to the ground, exhausted but alive. Alex and Lila rushed to his side, relief etched on their faces.

But even as they caught their breath, Tomas knew that this was just the beginning. The darkness they had been fighting was still out there, lurking in the shadows, waiting for its next opportunity to strike.

Tomas and his companions had to be ready - for whatever lay ahead.

Chapter 98

Tomas and his companions emerged from the forest, exhausted and shaken from the constant battles with
darkness. They had been on the run for weeks, searching for a way to destroy the malevolent force that seemed to be growing stronger by the day.
As they stumbled upon a small town, they hoped to find some reprieve. But as they walked the quiet streets, they
knew something was off. The town was deserted, and the air was thick with an eerie silence.
Tomas's intuition kicked in, and he knew they needed to be cautious. They crept into a nearby café, but the doors
slammed shut behind them, trapping them inside. The lights flickered, and the room filled with an ominous darkness.
Suddenly, a voice echoed through the room. "Welcome, Tomas," it said.
Tomas froze, recognizing the voice as belonging to the malevolent force they had been trying to destroy. He braced himself, waiting for the worst.
But then, a piercing light filled the room, and the darkness vanished. The group emerged from the café, blinking in the bright
sunlight.
As they walked down the deserted streets, Tomas knew that they were closer than ever to destroying the source of
the darkness. His intuition had never been stronger, and he knew that they were on the right track.

But what lay ahead would be their toughest challenge yet.

The darkness had grown too powerful, and they would need to be prepared for a battle unlike any they had faced before.

Chapter 99

Tomas and his companions emerged from the café, blinking in the bright sunlight. They had been trapped

inside for days, their supplies dwindling and their spirits
dampened by the oppressive force that surrounded them.

But now, with the sun shining down on them once more, they felt renewed.
As they walked through the deserted streets, they noticed something odd. The
buildings were all pristine, as though they had never been touched by human
hands. The
windows were clean, the doors unblemished, and the sidewalks were free of
any debris.
Tomas stopped in his tracks and squinted at a nearby storefront. "This isn't
right," he muttered, his intuition telling him that something was off.
Alex and Lila looked at him, their eyes questioning. Tomas gestured towards
the building. "Look at it. It's like it's been
frozen in time. There's no dust, no wear and tear. It's like it's pristine."
The group continued walking, their unease growing with each passing moment. As they turned a corner, they saw a figure in the
distance. It was a woman, dressed in white, her hair
flowing behind her in the breeze. She was walking towards them, her eyes fixed
on Tomas.
As she approached, Tomas felt a sense of dread wash over him. He knew that
this woman was not what she seemed.
Before he could react, the woman lunged at him, her hands grasping for his
throat. Tomas fought back, his training

and intuition guiding his every move. He managed to break free, but the woman was relentless, her attacks quick and vicious.

Alex and Lila rushed to his aid, their own weapons drawn.

Together, the group battled the possessed woman, their strength and determination keeping them alive.

Finally, with a powerful swing of his sword, Tomas struck the woman down. She fell to the ground, her body limp and lifeless.

Breathing heavily, the group looked at each other, knowing that they had just narrowly escaped death once again. They knew that there was still a long way to go before they

would be able to vanquish the darkness, but they were determined to see it through.

With renewed vigor, Tomas, Alex, and Lila set off down the deserted streets, ready to face whatever other horrors lay ahead.

Chapter 100

As Tomas and his companions walked towards the outskirts of the town, they noticed a figure standing in the distance. It was a woman, dressed in a long, flowing white gown. Her dark hair cascaded down her back, and her eyes glowed in the fading light.

Tomas approached her cautiously, his intuition telling him that she was different from anyone they had encountered on their journey. As he drew closer, she smiled warmly at him, and he felt a sense of calm wash over him.

"Welcome," she said, her voice soft and melodic. "I've been expecting you."

Tomas and his companions exchanged a puzzled look, but the woman didn't seem to notice.

"My name is Sophia," she continued. "I've been waiting for someone like you to come along and help me banish the darkness that has taken hold of this town."

Tomas felt a surge of hope inside him. Could this woman be the key to their success? He trusted his intuition, and it told him that she was a force for good.

Sophia led them to a building at the edge of town, where they found a group of people huddled together, terrified and hopeless.

"We've been hiding here for days," one of them said.

"We've been hearing strange noises and seeing things moving in the shadows."

Tomas and his companions knew that they had to act fast.

With Sophia's help, they began to devise a plan to banish the darkness once and for all.

As they made their way through the deserted streets, they encountered more possessed beings, but with Sophia's guidance, they were able to defeat them quickly and efficiently.

Finally, they reached the source of the darkness - a dark, foreboding mansion at the edge of town. With Sophia's
help, they entered the mansion and found themselves face-to-face with the cloaked figures they had encountered before.
But this time, they were ready. With a wave of Sophia's hand, a bright light filled the room, banishing the darkness and revealing the true identity of the cloaked figures priests from a nearby church who had been corrupted by the darkness.
Tomas and his companions emerged from the mansion victorious, knowing that they had banished the darkness
that had plagued the town for so long. Sophia thanked them for their help and disappeared into the night.
Tomas couldn't shake the feeling that he had met her before, but he couldn't quite place where. He knew,
however, that his intuition had led him to her, and that without it, he would never have been able to defeat the darkness.
As he and his companions walked away from the town,
Tomas felt a sense of accomplishment and pride. He had followed his intuition to the very end, and it had led him to victory.

Did you love *Power Of Intuition*? Then you should read *The Wise Monkey*[1] by Hash Blink and Thomas sheriff!

[2]

Certainly! To elaborate on the text provided, let me expand on the setting, characters' emotions, and the plot to provide more detail and context in a paragraph format.

As dawn's first light pierced the dense forest canopy, Ling, the wise monkey, and his stalwart friends found themselves on the precipice of the mystical Hidden Grove. The air around them was thick with a sense of anticipation, the kind that precedes moments of great importance. Despite the beauty that met their eyes, a profound sadness seemed to grip the once teeming sanctuary of green. The trees, those ancient sentinels of wisdom, now stood gaunt and bare, like mournful spirits against the sky.

1. https://books2read.com/u/bM2aG7

2. https://books2read.com/u/bM2aG7

As they trudged into the grove, their every step seemed to echo with the weight of responsibility they bore. For each of them, the journey had been long, fraught with doubts and the shadows of fear. Yet, in the company of one another, those fears had been alchemized into a shared resolve, a resolute purpose to heal the lands they called home. The silence of the forest was punctuated only by the rustlings of the remaining creatures, who watched with cautious eyes, their futures resting upon the courage of these unlikely heroes.

Ling and his friends could not help but pause and reflect on the trials they had faced, the growth each had undergone as individuals and as a united front. They were no longer mere inhabitants of the forest; they had become its fierce protectors, guardians chosen to confront the encroaching darkness that sought to rend the delicate fabric of their world. Ling felt the weight of their past triumphs and knew that the challenges ahead would ask more of them than ever before.

Amidst the quietude, a voice as serene as a gentle brook yet as powerful as the rush of a waterfall spoke from the depths of the grove. It was Alia, the Enchanted Keeper, her face an embodiment of tranquility, her eyes holding the depth of oceans. She emerged like a vision, her form a manifestation of the forest's cries and hopes. Her soft words carried a sense of urgency, reminding Ling and his companions of the formidable test that lay ahead—the final confrontation with the darkness that had cast its pall over the realm.

The companions felt an invigorating energy surge through them as they drew closer to Alia. She reminded them of their humble beginnings, the seeds of bravery they had sown, and the unity that had blossomed among them. It was this unity, Alia proclaimed, that would be their greatest weapon, a force that no shadow could withstand. With a knowing nod, she beckoned them forth, signaling the beginning of the final leg of their journey.

Ling, with a determined glint in his eyes, led the march towards their fateful destination. The path before them was shrouded in uncertainty, but the bonds they had formed, tempered by adversity and kindled by mutual trust, illuminated the way. Their hearts, though weary, were undaunted, for they had learned that even the smallest glimmer of hope could banish the deepest darkness.

As the gentle light of dawn turned to the golden hues of day, Ling and his companions journeyed on, each step a testament to their unwavering resolve. Their tale—a chronicle of courage, friendship, and the eternal quest for harmony—would echo through the forest for generations to come, a legacy born from the indomitable spirit of the wise monkey and his friends.

Also by Hash Blink

POWER
Power Of Intuition

Standalone
The zodiac sign lover's
Hades
The immortal lover
The Wise Monkey
The forbidden idol

Watch for more at https://books.apple.com/us/audiobook/the-power-of-the-loner-discover-the/id1727418972.

Also by Thomas sheriff

POWER
Power Of Intuition

Standalone
The immortal lover
The Wise Monkey
The forbidden idol

Watch for more at https://books.apple.com/us/audiobook/the-male-hierar-chy/id1727414547.

About the Author

Hash Blink, born Thomas B. Sherriff, is a hip hop artist and storyteller. With a global perspective shaped by his Liberian roots and his experiences in the vibrant hip-hop scene of Chicago, Hash Blink's music and literature transcend boundaries and captivate audiences.

Read more at https://books.apple.com/us/audiobook/the-power-of-the-loner-discover-the/id1727418972.

About the Publisher

Hi, I'm the founder of Hash Blink & Rebellious Rebels LLC and a book writer. I've always been passionate about technology, and that's why I started Hash Blink & Rebellious Rebels LLC - to make it easier for people to find all the entertainment online. I also love writing books and exploring the world of literature. My mission is to create stories that inspire readers to think differently about the world around them. Through my work, I hope to bring more knowledge and understanding into our lives.

Milton Keynes UK
Ingram Content Group UK Ltd.
UKHW010641040324
438885UK00001B/192